LISTEN TO THE STARS

Six spellbinding stories

Avi Mukherjee

LISTEN TO THE STARS
SIX SPELLBINDING STORIES

Copyright © 2023 Avi Mukherjee.

All rights reserved. No part of this book may be used or reproduced by any means, graphic, electronic, or mechanical, including photocopying, recording, taping or by any information storage retrieval system without the written permission of the author except in the case of brief quotations embodied in critical articles and reviews.

This is a work of fiction. All of the characters, names, incidents, organizations, and dialogue in this novel are either the products of the author's imagination or are used fictitiously.

iUniverse books may be ordered through booksellers or by contacting:

iUniverse
1663 Liberty Drive
Bloomington, IN 47403
www.iuniverse.com
844-349-9409

Because of the dynamic nature of the Internet, any web addresses or links contained in this book may have changed since publication and may no longer be valid. The views expressed in this work are solely those of the author and do not necessarily reflect the views of the publisher, and the publisher hereby disclaims any responsibility for them.

Any people depicted in stock imagery provided by Getty Images are models, and such images are being used for illustrative purposes only. Certain stock imagery © Getty Images.

ISBN: 978-1-6632-5033-9 (sc)
ISBN: 978-1-6632-5035-3 (hc)
ISBN: 978-1-6632-5034-6 (e)

Library of Congress Control Number: 2023901619

Print information available on the last page.

iUniverse rev. date: 02/27/2023

CONTENTS

Flow with the Tide..1

In ***Flow with the Tide***, set mostly in Japan, we join the desperate search of a young girl for her American marine father who does not believe that she is his daughter.

Another World...33

Then we enter ***Another World***, the exciting world of high stakes poker and the characters who inhabit it. Many of us are familiar with TV poker shows, but few know how poker players deal with the conflicts between an unconventional sport and a more conventional lifestyle.

Never Alone..57

Never Alone is the startling, poignant and often shocking story of a mentally ill son, told by the father. It is at the same time a deeply personal story and a criticism of our society's handling of the mentally ill. They are the marginalized among us, but they don't have to be.

Click for Romance...89

Online dating has its rewards, hazards, and a funny side. In ***Click for Romance***, we see different sides of the online dating scene through the true-to-life experiences of an American businessman.

Smile without Reason 115

Although Covid-19 is almost behind us, there may be more deadly virus pandemics in the future. ***Smile without Reason*** cleverly explores a scary futuristic scenario, while also making a case against tampering with genes and viruses, ostensibly for the benefit of mankind.

Listen to the Stars 147

In ***Listen to the Stars***, we are exposed to fascinating perspectives about the universe and humanity, about life and death, and about philosophy and religion.

FLOW WITH THE TIDE

We know not from whence the tide comes or whither it goes

What an irony! mused Cesar, as he went to bed that night. Only a month into his assignment in Tokyo, he was strongly attracted to a Japanese girl who he could not have a relationship with because she was emigrating to the US in a few months while he, who was from the US, was going to be stuck in Japan for the next few years. As if that wasn't enough, she was depending on him to make her life's goal a reality.

"Interested in an assignment to Tokyo?", his boss at Goldman Sachs had asked him five months ago.

"Sure, when do I leave?" replied Cesar with a laugh.

It was a hectic two months of preparation and Cesar had never felt so excited. After his divorce, with no children, he was beginning to tire of Manhattan and had always wanted to visit Japan. It was a perfect opportunity, not just for experiencing a new country and culture, but also from the standpoint of professional advancement in one of Goldman Sachs' premier international offices.

He started taking Japanese language lessons within a few weeks of his settling down. Although he could say a few words by now, corresponding to *good morning* or *good afternoon* or *how are you*, it was a daunting task to become familiar enough with the language to feel comfortable in strange surroundings. Just the day before, his language teacher, Mr. Seiki, whom everyone called Seiki-sensei (*sensei* is the Japanese word for teacher), asked Cesar during a break if he was married. When Cesar said he was recently divorced, Seiki-sensei said to him,

"You good-looking with friendly face, nice smile. Japanese girls will like you. Go, find Japanese girlfriend! That is fast way to learn Japanese!"

Cesar laughed and replied, "Easy to say",

Seiki-sensei urged "*Gambatte*", Do your best!"

Cesar knew in his heart that Seiki-sensei was right; it was a long time since he had last dated a woman, and even then, never an Asian woman.

Lunchtime on a weekday in Tokyo is always full of crammed sidewalks, busy with office workers hurriedly going to lunch. That midsummer day was characteristically warm, with a few drops of rain from scattered clouds. Cesar walked with the crowd, not quite decided on where to go for lunch. There were so many choices in Tokyo that every day was an adventure. Tokyo has three times as many restaurants as London and New York City combined, a startling statistic that allows one to go to a different place for lunch every day of the year if one wanted to, all within a few minutes' walk from the office.

Cesar was determined to find a new place for lunch that day. *It is easier than finding a girlfriend*, he thought, as he got off the subway at Nakameguro, which was a nearby neighborhood to his office in Roppongi, easily accessible by one of the subway lines. Roppongi was too full of foreigners and was sorely lacking in quaint places for lunch. He always looked for signs on restaurants with English words as indicators that there would be English on the menu. There was no need for the staff to be English speaking. As long as the menu was in English, he could always point to an item. Of course, there was always the Denny's or McDonald's or Tony Roma's to fall back on, but it would be a shame when there were so many other delectable choices on the streets of Tokyo.

Walking the narrow streets near the Nakameguro subway station, he saw a sign that read *Coffee and Snacks/Mon Petit*. There were pictures of 'set' lunches, where one just chooses A, B, or C and gets a tray set with two or three different items. The concept of custom orders is not common, especially for lunch. Encouraged by the sign, Cesar entered, was seated and was handed the menu. The menu did have pictures, but *there was no English*. Cesar felt cheated because the sign outside was in English and partially in French. He was in trouble.

The waiter came and asked him something which he didn't understand. He looked around and saw a pretty girl, Eurasian very likely, in her mid to late twenties, sitting by herself at an adjacent table, reading a Japanese magazine. She had long dark brown hair hanging straight down on both sides of her pale oval face. No makeup. No necklace or earrings. A typical office lady, *Office Flowers* they are called in Japan, one of thousands in every neighborhood. Yet, she seemed special, if only because of her looks. Not Japanese, not Caucasian, somewhere in between. *Eurasians are so uniquely pretty*, Cesar said to himself. Maybe she knew a little English! She was two tables away from him sitting facing in his direction. Suddenly she looked up, as if sensing she was being stared at. She caught his eye, but he quickly looked away, embarrassed, and tried to study the menu, making sure that he was holding it right side up! Out of the corner of his eye, he felt she was looking at him, sensing his inability to comprehend the menu, with the waiter hovering impatiently near him. This time he looked up more boldly in her direction, and she smiled at him and asked,

"Can I help with menu?" Cesar felt his pulse quicken in a way he had not felt in years.

"Yes please", he said wondering why his voice sounded so dry. This was Japan, this girl was pretty, she spoke English, and seemed friendly. "*Find Japanese girlfriend!*", the words of Seiki-sensei, although in imperfect English, resounded at the back of his head, as he watched her move over to the empty chair across from him.

Her name was Annie. After the ordeal of ordering lunch was over, Cesar told her about his job, his new assignment in Tokyo, his difficulties with the language, and that he was divorced. He explained that his assignment would nominally be for three years, but definitely less than five. Annie had spent a year staying with friends in Santa Monica, California, a couple of years ago, and that was where she had picked up a little English. Cesar instinctively felt that she liked him, and he definitely liked her. By the time their introductions were completed, lunch was over, and it was time to get back to work. Cesar asked for her mobile number and Annie quickly obliged. As they got up to leave, Annie said

"I will tell you more next time, and I may need your help".

With that enigmatic parting line, she quickly walked out of the narrow door of the restaurant, and disappeared into the crowded streets of Nakameguro. Cesar, walking with a light but jaunty step, her phone number securely in his wallet, the *next time* ringing pleasantly in his ears, took the short subway ride back to his office in Mori Towers, Roppongi.

That evening, Cesar decided to go to a jazz club close to his apartment. Jazz helped him relax and think about life, philosophy, the interplay between work and enjoyment, between rigor and relaxation, between money and music, and between celibacy and relationships. Single-malt scotch went well with jazz and Cesar indulged in both. Annie was on his mind. Although their meeting was brief, she had affected him strangely and strongly. *I will tell you more next time, and I may need your help.* He wondered how she thought he could possibly help her. All she knew about him was that he was an American, on a job assignment in Tokyo. She had given him her number, but she did not ask for or have his. He was inherently shy and not the type of guy who could easily ask women out for dates. Many a time, in his youth, he had regretted missed opportunities. *Well*, thought Cesar, *the next meeting should be quite interesting.* The jazz club was busy. Most of the patrons were Japanese and were enjoying the music. *Jazz is alive and well in Tokyo*, thought Cesar, while sipping his Oban 21 single malt and listening to the young guest musician from Los Angeles crooning *You are too beautiful*. Cesar let the soft romantic music merge melodically with his thoughts.

He called Annie a few days later to ask her out to dinner, and Annie accepted. She wanted to go to a quiet place, and suggested a Western restaurant since Japanese restaurants were typically crowded and noisy. As soon as the call was over, Cesar hummed one of his favorite tunes and did a little pirouette, happy that the next phase with Annie was about to begin.

The hours dragged by too slowly for Cesar until the dinner date. He dressed well, knowing that Japanese women liked to dress up for any outing, and definitely for dinner. He ran down the stairs to the subway and got on a train just before the doors slammed shut. He looked forward to a nice chat over dinner, but could never have guessed that over dinner Annie would tell him such a fascinating story, the story of her life.

Annie was born in Okinawa, the daughter of Jonathan, an American marine, and Sayoko, her Japanese mother. Okinawa is one of the South Sea islands in the Ryukyu islands chain near southern Japan, well known as an American naval base. Sayoko was deeply in love with Jonathan, and they were together for just over six months when he had to go back to the States, temporarily, he told her. She was pregnant with Annie, but she did not tell him she was pregnant, intending to surprise him with the good news on his return. Unfortunately, for one reason or another, Jonathan never returned to Okinawa.

Sayoko tried to contact him but failed. Her English ability was limited, so she could not directly call the US Marine offices to find out his whereabouts. His mobile number was no longer in service and her letters to his known address were returned, addressee unknown. Her pride was terribly hurt that he did not try to contact her, and it ended up that she never got to tell him about Annie. She felt lonely and hurt, carrying the baby of a man who had disappeared into nowhere and whom she may never see again. She knew this could happen, from the experiences of others, but never thought that it would happen between her and Jonathan. Soon after Annie was born, she met and married Larry, another American serviceman.

Annie's eyes glistened as she told her story. Cesar listened without interruption. Annie spoke with an intensity and a sense of urgency that Cesar found fascinating, and she also portrayed a maturity that belied her age. Soon after her mother married Larry, they emigrated to the US, leaving Annie with her aunt in Okinawa, who legitimized her by giving her their family name, Tamashiro, and raised her with her other children as one of her own. Annie, who never knew her father, was separated from her birth mother when she was less than a year old. It was not until she was eight years old that her aunt told her that her mother was married to an American, and living in the USA and her mother had tried but could never contact her biological father after she was born.

"Although I loved my aunt just same as own mother, from the day I knew she not real mother, I feel very strange, I start dislike my real mother, who leave me, but I determined to meet her and then find my father. That was dream of little girl Annie. Today, I am a little bit closer to my dream, but I will explain more later". Annie paused and looked at her watch.

Dinner was long over and the patrons were leaving the restaurant one group at a time. Time had flown, realized Cesar, but he wanted to listen to the rest of her story. Cesar had never heard a story like this and said softly, "Let us order some dessert and tea, I would like to hear more".

"My first letter to Sayoko was written with aunt help. I still remember how I start that letter. My first words were *Mom, I am your daughter, Annie. Please write me back.*"

Annie broke down as she said this, and Cesar turned his face. He had not felt tears well into his eyes like this in a long time. A couple sitting at the next table shot them a quick glance then looked away. Annie pulled herself together and continued:

"Sayoko and I began write to each other and Sayoko told me story of Jonathan and herself. Sayoko wrote to me that soon after reaching the States, she wrote again to Jonathan and told him about me. This time Jonathan reply, but told her he did not believe her, because she never told him she was expecting. Jonathan suspicious that my mother was pretend that her baby was Jonathan's. Jonathan told her he married and had family, and wished to be left alone. Sayoko considered going through legal system to get child support from Jonathan, but her husband said *no* because too stressful and may not be success anyway. In one of my letters to my mother, I asked her how I could find Jonathan? She had no idea. Almost ten years had passed, and my mother had completely lost track of Jonathan."

Cesar noticed that Annie was sometimes referring to her mother by her name, Sayoko, and at other times referring to her as *my mother*. He connected this to her being not that close to her mother while growing up, in fact not knowing her at all until she was eight.

"After finishing high school in Okinawa, I got an administrative job in Tokyo, the work I am doing now, and after a couple of years, I took some time off to visit friends in Santa Monica. I used the opportunity to meet my mother who I think of more as an older friend, not really a mother. I had hard time to think of Sayoko as my mother because I could not accept that my mother would leave me behind in Okinawa and go to live in the USA. Do you understand me?" Annie said, looking into Cesar's eyes.

Cesar correctly read that as meaning *Can you empathize with my feelings*?

"Yes, I understand",

Annie continued after a brief pause.

"Larry and Sayoko moved to Las Vegas. Larry had job in casino and Sayoko was Japanese teacher in local high school. I did not care much for Sayoko or Larry. I felt that my life would be so much better if I could just find my father and meet *him*. At least my father hadn't abandoned *me*. He had left Sayoko without knowing about me. I even felt sorry for Jonathan because I didn't like my mother either. I have to find my father. I would not ask anything of him. Just accept me. During my baby years, whenever I needed comforting, I wished my father was there for me. All my friends at school had fathers. Why did I not have one? I could not fully figure out. Sayoko gave me a picture of my father which is my most treasured possession". Annie reached into her bag, saying,

"I normally don't carry this around. I took it out of safe deposit at bank to show you. This is my father. Isn't he handsome?".

Cesar felt honored. He was looking at a black and white picture of the face of a handsome young man, with an attractive smile, wearing a marine uniform. At the back there was a heart drawn in red ink with the words, *With Love from Jonathan* written underneath.

During Annie's visit to Las Vegas, Larry and her mother told her they would help her emigrate to the US. Now, two and a half years later, Annie's application for permanent residency in the US had been approved and she was just waiting for the final papers. As soon as she got them, she would go over and stay with either Larry and Sayoko, or with her friend in Santa Monica. However, she would have to find her father on her own. She couldn't expect much help from Larry or her mother. Then she looked at Cesar, straight into his eyes,

"Can you help me find my father?"

Cesar was taken aback. So, this explained the cryptic comment she had made the first night as she was leaving after lunch.

"But how can I help?"

"You can call and ask US Government where is he. At least you will be lot better than me, with my poor English! You can tell them you are his daughter's friend and his daughter is searching for him, or something like that, can you please? You are only American I know in Tokyo. In office where I work, and where I live, there are not many foreigners."

Annie looked expectantly at Cesar. Cesar could not help reaching across the table and laying his hand gently on Annie's, expressing, in one touch, the complexities of friendship, understanding, support and togetherness.

"Yes, you are right. OK, I will try my best."

With that, they both realized that the evening had come to an end, and it was time to leave.

As they walked out the door, into the warm summer night, Cesar drew her close and touched her cheek to his. He felt a slight resistance on her part, a slight stiffening, which was understandable since this was their first experience at closeness. It was almost midnight and Annie went down the subway stairs at the crosswalk close to the restaurant, in time to catch the last train. Cesar walked the mile or so to his apartment, mingling with the late-night crowd, midnight revelers, office workers going home after visiting their favorite restaurants and bars, tourists taking pictures and couples walking hand in hand. Many different emotions filled his mind: Happiness and expectation from making a new female acquaintance, nervousness at the task he had undertaken and the risk of failure, responsibility that he had been shouldered with, and finally the challenge of finding a lost father. What a story this frail little girl had just shared with him!

Annie's story kept going through his mind, but even more so, he remembered the details of Annie's intense expression, her moist eyes, her attempts at expressing complex emotions in a language she was not so good at, the touch of her cheek against his and her poignant request to him, *"Can you help me find my father?"* As Cesar looked up at the tall chrome and glass office buildings on either side of the street with the lighted and dark windows forming a crossword puzzle type patchwork, he wondered if there were other fascinating stories behind each window. A big city has millions of people and millions of stories, and tonight he had just heard one of them.

One of Cesar's colleagues, Kato, a Japanese American, was quite familiar with both cultures and was one of Cesar's closest buddies and confidantes. Kato's wife was Japanese and they often invited Cesar for dinner at their apartment in the upscale neighborhood of Minami Azabu, not too far from Roppongi. The night after he heard Annie's story, he was invited to dinner, and over dinner he told them about Annie. They were as moved as Cesar was, and the three of them discussed how to proceed in locating the whereabouts of Annie's father. They found a few phone numbers online for US Marine Headquarters in the US and also in Okinawa, and Cesar jotted them down. They also tried to find Jonathan's name in standard online searches for people, but drew a blank. There seemed to be no one within the right age range. It was not going to be an easy task, realized Cesar, but he was willing to try. Kato said he was surprised Annie told him so much about her life. It was not typical for a Japanese woman to be so open so early after meeting someone. However, Kato's wife pointed out that Annie was probably not a typical Japanese woman, because of her background, and also there seemed to be a level of urgency in her quest, which probably prompted her to be so open with Cesar. In any case, Cesar admitted that he felt a strong liking for Annie, but was not sure how to go forward given her vulnerability and the fact that she seemed to want to depend on him for this task she had given him. When he was leaving, Kato's wife said,

"Annie is like a precious pearl for you, the pearl of Okinawa! Let things take their course, just *flow with the tide* and see where it takes you, see if there is a pearl at the end". *Seems like a reasonable plan*, thought Cesar.

Over the next couple of days Cesar called different US Government, US Navy and Marines numbers in the US. He had to reschedule some clients to afternoon meetings, since the only time window for calling the US was very early morning. It was a forbidding task, since most of the time he didn't get much more than a recorded voice or instructions to call other numbers. On the few occasions he connected with a live human, he had to give long explanations of who he was and why he was trying to locate Jonathan. Cesar was not one to give up. Somewhere in the back of his mind, there was the expectation that he would be able to get closer to Annie if he made progress in the task which she had entrusted him with. Also, he felt good that he was helping someone who was so desperately in need. He knew from Annie that Jonathan's home town was Chicago, so his next plan was to focus there.

He decided to ask Annie out that weekend and planned to spend the day with her after lunch, although he had not made much progress in finding Jonathan. Annie accepted, and they agreed to meet at the entrance to the Meiji shrine, next to Harajuku Station. Cesar went there quite early. Harajuku is internationally known as a center for Japanese youth fashion. Cesar enjoyed hanging around Harajuku on weekends, watching the young men and women often dressed in incongruous, outdated and comical styles; the women with faces painted, garish lip colors and hairdos in all shapes and colors except their own natural black or dark brown. It was like an outdoor Halloween costume party somehow transfused into real life, spanning about four or five blocks, going on pretty much every day, and more intensely on weekends. Cesar was always struck by the fact that the Meiji shrine grounds are a stark contrast in every possible way to the Harajuku scene right next door. One may as well be on a different planet. A huge expanse of tall trees and forested land, spanning over one hundred and fifty acres, affording Tokyoites with a place to relax, contemplate and reflect, with no car or office building in sight. One need not walk all the way to the shrine itself to be overcome by a sense of serenity and peacefulness, being practically a million miles away from the bustling megalopolis that is Tokyo.

Cesar was well aware that not everyone liked or respected the Meiji shrine. It is a relatively recently constructed Shinto shrine, a memorial to Emperor Meiji and to imperial Japan. Although Cesar was a Catholic by birth, his parents had taught him tolerance and respect for all religions. He was fascinated by Buddhism and had recently been reading up on Shintoism which was uniquely Japanese and associated with imperialism in many people's minds, although it was a coincidental association. Modern day Japanese believe more in democracy than imperialism, and the emperor is little more than a figurehead. Cesar couldn't care less. Irrespective of the history of the shrine, he was going to spend the afternoon walking with

Annie on the idyllic shrine grounds, and he hoped to get closer to her. Kato's wife's words were on his mind. *Just flow with the tide,* she had said.

Cesar was standing in front of the entrance to the Meiji shrine grounds, looking at the throng of people exiting the Japan Rail station, searching anxiously for Annie, when suddenly there was a tap on his shoulder. He turned quickly around thinking that Annie may be trying to catch him by surprise. It was not her. Instead, it was one of the Harajuku girls, a garishly outfitted teenager. "*Konnichiwa*", she said. Cesar knew it meant *Good Day* and replied "*Konnichiwa*". The girl assumed he knew Japanese, and there was a torrent of words with a questioning look at the end. Cesar realized the mistake he had made in replying in Japanese. He crossed his hands in front of his chest, and said "*Nihongo*". Nihongo is the Japanese word for the Japanese language, and the crossed hands meant *I don't know Japanese.* This is standard sign language when there is failed communication between a Japanese and a foreigner. The girl understood, and was walking away when Annie showed up. Seeing Annie, she got fresh courage, and they exchanged a few words in Japanese. She handed Annie a card and walked away. Annie smiled at him and said,

"Hi Cesar, wait long"?

Annie was dressed in a white shirt, with a beige and dark brown plaid skirt. She looked beautiful and elegant. Her medium length dark brown hair fell straight on both sides of her face, and some stray strands shone in the sunlight coming from an angle. *Annie looks so gorgeous,* thought Cesar and it made him nervous and shy.

"I was just walking around Harajuku, watching people for the past half hour. What was that girl saying?"

"Oh, she advertising blind date meeting place for singles. Tokyo has many places where singles can go and talk from separate cubicles and meet face to face only if both want to. I was no interest, so she just gave me business card".

Cesar had heard of such places from his friend Kato, but not knowing Japanese, had never dared to seek them out.

Walking side by side, not holding hands yet, Cesar told Annie about his lack of progress in locating Jonathan.

"Oh, that is OK, I not expect anything so quick".

"I will try Chicago next".

Annie suddenly stopped walking and looked at Cesar,

"You know something, one of his hobbies was playing darts and he competed in darts tournament, my mother told me. Maybe that help!"

Cesar nodded, filing away that piece of information.

"Any little thing that you can remember about Jonathan may help, indeed!"

They kept walking down the wide path that wound its way between the tall trees and led towards the shrine. They had both visited the Meiji shrine before, so the shrine itself was of little interest to them, but the walk up to the shrine was always full of novelty. The trees looked different in different seasons, the people were different, the birds were different and flew different routes, and of course the sky and air were different every day. There were many couples walking hand in hand. Cesar wondered about him and Annie. They looked exactly like a couple, but they were not, at least not yet. They saw an empty bench and Cesar made a move towards it, Annie followed and they sat down. Cesar sat close to Annie and gently put his arm around her shoulders.

Annie didn't say anything for a few seconds. Then she looked at him, "Cesar, I must tell you something. I like you very much but we can't have relationship. I not belong here in Tokyo no more. I on my way to living in USA. You have to stay here for few years and work here. This is not good situation to start relationship."

Cesar was struck by her directness. She must have sensed his liking for her. The irony of what Annie had just told him was not lost on him. He, an American, was being denied a closer relationship with an attractive Japanese woman because he was forced to live in Japan and she was on her way to living in the USA! On the other hand, they would perhaps not even have met if their situations were any different. *The strange vagaries of life*, thought Cesar.

"Of course, I understand", he said and Annie continued,

"If you not mind, I very much like you to be my friend for now, and I still want your help with finding my father. I think my life change for better if I could meet him".

Cesar gave her a hug. She hugged him back and then they just sat there for a while in silence.

After a while, Annie started talking about her mother.

"My mother was pretty woman, but very stupid! After short romance with a Japanese high school boyfriend, she was determined to date only white men".

"How come?"

"Well, in mother's generation, and even now, Japanese women strongly like white men. Long before American servicemen were in Okinawa, the only white people that Okinawans were exposed to were in Hollywood movies. My mother told me stories about how she thought John Wayne was godlike in appearance: tall, blue eyes, sexy smile, ten-gallon hat. Then, when John Wayne look-alikes came to Okinawa, there was no resisting them, even though they not exactly look-alikes. They could have their way with almost any Japanese woman they chose, and they did. Don't you think my mother was stupid?".

"Well, I can understand the fascination with Western men in a culture that has been isolated from the West for a very long time. I wouldn't call her stupid, just misguided".

Annie was not familiar with the word *misguided* so Cesar patiently explained to her the difference between *stupid* and *misguided.*

"You can be my English teacher!" said Annie.

"Yes, and will you pay me?"

Annie shot back, "Only half the going rate, just for me, OK?"

Cesar laughed. Teaching English in Japan was a lucrative profession. He knew several young Americans, Britishers, Canadians, Australians and New Zealanders who were making between four to six thousand US dollars a month just teaching English.

"My mother never took English lessons until she went to US with Larry, but now, living in English-speaking environment, her listening and speaking is fairly good, but she still cannot write at all."

"So, how did she communicate with your father?"

"Oh, she wrote in Japanese and Jonathan had it translated and vice versa", said Annie.

Some children near them squealed suddenly as a lone pigeon flew close to them. They threw some pigeon feed on the side of the pathway and suddenly close to twenty pigeons appeared as if from nowhere. A small gathering of children and their parents stood watching the pigeons eat, and were taking pictures with their phones and cameras.

"It's part of ritual of visiting shrine", Annie told Cesar.

Soon the pigeons dispersed, and the children and their parents continued on their way to the shrine, disappearing from view where the path curved between the stately trees about a hundred feet from where they sat.

Sometimes Annie spoke with her head bent forward, and when she did, Cesar could not see her full face, with her hair covering it partially from his view, enhancing the mystery of her story.

Suddenly she asked,

"Cesar, are you really happy that you had mother and father while growing up?"

It was a question that took him by surprise, a topic that Cesar had never really thought much about. Everyone he knew had parents, unless of course they had passed away. There were many things about his parents that he did not care for, but overall, he felt he had a happy childhood because he understood them, understood where they were coming from, and accepted his fate of having them as his parents. It really wasn't so bad. They were the only people who unselfishly cared for him, and he had no other choice. He was never unhappy with them as people. Perhaps he was sometimes unhappy with the way they behaved towards him, but that was temporary. As these thoughts were going through his head, he realized how different and difficult it must have been for Annie, to grow up with other kids, all of whom had parents, and she was different.

"Well, I was happy overall, I must say, but I realize it must have been difficult for you?".

Annie's response surprised Cesar.

"Most kids around me complained about their parents. Until I was eight years old, I thought my aunt and uncle were my parents and they were really so nice to me. So, I thought I very lucky to have such nice parents while most of my classmates only talked about how evil their parents were!"

Cesar wanted to ask her, *what were your thoughts after you found out about your real parents from your aunt?* They were quiet for a while, and listened to the background talk and laughter of the people, young and old, Japanese and foreigners, who strolled past them on their way to the Meiji shrine, with their feet crunching the gravel as they walked, and the occasional piercing shriek of a little girl or boy, surprised by one of the pigeons flying around.

Finally, Annie answered the question on Cesar's mind.

"When I found out about my real parents, at first I just didn't know what to think. It was as if bottom fall out of my world, but then I very quickly realized I was much more mature and experienced than any kids around me. I realized I capable of deeper thought and more complicated emotions and at the same time able to have simple and clear plan for my future. While parents of other kids wanted them to do well at school with some future career goal in mind, my goal was simple, find my mother and then my father. I lucky to have such clear and desirable goal which no one could question, no one could argue with, ever!"

Annie's words stunned Cesar, not so much by their simplicity or pathos but because they placed him squarely in a position to impact her life's goal, which she had decided for herself from the tender age of eight. The late afternoon sun cast long shadows of the trees on the shrine grounds. The sky was still clear but a few dark clouds could be seen planning to block the sun within a few minutes. Cesar got up to stretch his legs,

"Shall we walk towards the shrine?".

They slowly walked the quarter mile or so (half a kilometer, in metric Japan) to the shrine. When they reached it, Annie went to one of the shops that lined the courtyard and bought a couple of small wooden plates and a felt tipped pen.

"This shrine has special place for writing and keeping any wish you have. There is divine power that people believe will grant them any reasonable wish. Just write it on this little wooden plate, it's called *ema* in Japanese, and place it over there",

Annie pointed to a board with numerous plates pinned to it. She herself wrote something in Japanese and hung the piece of wood on one of the pins on the board, which was overflowing with hanging plates.

"What did you wish for?"

"I wished that meeting you will help me find my father".

Cesar wrote his wish, and placed it next to Annie's. He wrote, *I wish Annie's wish comes true, and I can help her find her father.*

It was close to sunset, closing time, and they walked back out the way they had entered, out into the busy streets of Harajuku, leaving behind them the tranquil forested world of the Meiji shrine and their wishes written on small wooden plates, pinned to a board near the shrine.

The next few days Cesar was busy with work, but after the day's work was done, he planned the calls he would make to the US the next morning. Early in the morning, he would call the numbers, hoping to get a clue as to Jonathan's whereabouts. It was a difficult task at best, frustrating at worst. Some days Cesar just did not feel like trying any more, and on those days he felt guilty. Every call he made seemed to get him more involved. As he repeated the same words again and again, they became more real, more sincere: *I am a close friend of Annie and she has asked me to help her find her father*, was the refrain in every call. The Chicago area had several navy and marine offices, but Cesar was getting nowhere until he suddenly decided to call some Darts clubs and Darts competition information boards. He found several Darts clubs and Darts leagues, but no one seemed to know anyone by the name of Jonathan. Then, on the fourth day after they wrote their wishes on little wooden plates at the Meiji shrine, he struck paydirt. Windy City Darters, a big dart league, knew of Jonathan. He was a member of the league until a couple of years ago, but had not renewed his membership. Wendy, the secretary he talked with, told him that they did have his contact information but she could not give it to Cesar without Jonathan's permission. Cesar had to think quickly. If he told Wendy that he was a friend of Jonathan's daughter, he may never get anywhere because Jonathan would not be willing to communicate with a daughter whose very existence he doubted.

"I knew him from our time together as Marines in Okinawa, looking to find him after all these years!", lied Cesar.

"Please get his permission to give me his contact information".

Wendy asked Cesar his name and Cesar gave her his real name, confident that Jonathan would not remember everyone he knew many years ago. He hoped that Jonathan should be agreeable to talk to anyone from his Okinawa days, even if he didn't remember the name.

"OK", I will try to contact Jonathan. Give me your number and I can call you back".

Cesar gave her his US mobile number, but also said,

"I will call back in a couple of days if I haven't heard from you".

Two days passed by, with no call back from Wendy, then Cesar called the Windy City Darters number again. Wendy picked up and recognized his voice.

"Cesar, I have good news for you, Jonathan gave me permission to give you his number and email address."

Cesar felt his pulse quicken. His first thought was that Annie would be very happy to hear this.

"OK, please tell me".

He carefully wrote it down, then asked her to send it by email as a back-up. Cesar tried calling Annie at work that afternoon, planning to invite her to lunch the following day to give her the good news. She was not around, or had left for the day, it seemed. He left a message on her mobile, asking her to call him back. She called back late that evening, and they made a date for lunch the next day. Cesar wanted to see her face when he told her of the progress he had made. Annie suggested they meet at an Okinawan restaurant and sent him the address. Annie had said,

"Okinawa cuisine quite different from what majority of Tokyo people experience, and I want you taste it". Cesar had readily agreed.

That evening, Cesar went to the jazz club, and over a shot of Oban, listening to the music, he let his mind absorb the complexity of the situation he was getting into with Annie, and the mission to get her reunited with her father. He was beginning to play a central role now. *Would it be successful? Would it lead to something with Annie? What would be the next step? Would he have to contact Jonathan first? "Just flow with the tide…"* Kato's wife had advised. The whisky and the jazz made it easier to follow that advice, and Cesar slept well that night.

There was a light drizzle, so Cesar took a taxi to the restaurant. Japanese taxis are unique in that the door for passenger entry opens only on one side and is controlled by the driver. The passenger is not supposed to even touch the door, let alone open or shut it. Cesar always found this amusing. In his first few days in Tokyo, a taxi driver had told him that he could always tell a foreigner by his attempt at opening or shutting the cab door. The reverse was true in the US. Cab drivers would curse Japanese customers who left the cab with the door open, and the driver would have to get out of the cab to shut the door.

It was easy to spot Annie as he got off the taxi. She looked stunning in a red dress, wearing red lipstick, waiting for him with an off-white umbrella over her head, just outside the door of the restaurant. The color of the umbrella matched the paleness of her face. The restaurant was crowded and very full, but the owner knew Annie and had kept a table for them.

"I hope the rain doesn't last all day", said Cesar as he folded his umbrella and slipped it into a plastic sheath outside the entrance.

"Why, I love rain. It makes my day!" said Annie. Born and raised in Okinawa, she had grown up with rain and unlike most of her friends in Tokyo, eagerly waited for the enjoyment that a rainy day can bring.

It was the first time for Cesar in an Okinawan restaurant and he was impressed by its uniqueness. There were carved wooden masks hanging on the walls, which Annie explained were typical Okinawan handicraft. They reminded Cesar of similar masks he had seen in other Pacific islands, like Hawaii. The menu looked quite different from anything Cesar had seen elsewhere in Tokyo, and he let Annie order for him. Annie explained that many of the ingredients were brought in fresh from Okinawa almost daily.

"Okinawan food, like the special seaweed I ordered today, is very healthy. Did you know that Okinawa has the world's highest concentration of people over a hundred years old? My great grandmother and my grandmother both lived till their late nineties".

"So, you will live long too!"

"Nah, I left Okinawa long time; bad food and lifestyle here in Tokyo!"

Cesar waited to finish the meal. Then, over green tea, he told Annie the good news and the conversation he had with Wendy the previous day. Annie's excitement knew no bounds. She got up from her chair, walked across the table, hugged Cesar and kissed him on his cheek.

"Thank you. Thank you. Thank you!" she said.

Then she sat back down, looked him straight in the eye and asked, "What next?"

It was the same question that Cesar had pondered in the jazz club. Annie did not mince words:

"I need you to contact him and explain to him that I am really his daughter. Only you can do that".

Cesar had seen this coming. He had gotten deeply involved and there was no way out of doing exactly what she was asking. If Annie tried to contact Jonathan, he would just ignore her and not believe her story. He did not believe her mother, Sayoko, so why would he believe Annie? On the other hand, Cesar was even more of an outsider. How could Cesar be more persuasive?

"Well, let us think about how to proceed", was all he could say in response.

With that, it was time to get back to work. It was raining a bit harder and taxis are not easy to find when it rains in Tokyo. As you waved them in, you had to indicate with two outstretched fingers that you are willing to pay double the meter, to have any chance at getting a ride. They were lucky that someone got off in front of them and Annie ran and grabbed the taxi. Cesar couldn't be sure how many fingers were involved. He could feel her excitement and anticipation but also her doubts and uncertainty about the information he had just given her. Just before she got off at her work place, he placed his hand on hers,

"Don't worry, I will contact Jonathan, but let me think about the best way to do it".

She smiled and patted his hand back,

"I will wait to hear from you".

Then she got off the taxi, unfurled her umbrella and ran into her office building and back to work.

That evening Cesar went over to Kato's to get his and his wife's advice on how best to contact Jonathan. They agreed on Cesar sending a long email to Jonathan explaining how he had met Annie, heard Annie's story and offered to help her. He would explain that there was no doubt in his mind about her sincerity and no way she was not genuine, that she really loved him even though she had never met him. He would tell Jonathan that she carried around his picture, and had shown it to Cesar. She had a strong inner conviction that meeting him would change her life for the better. He could even do a paternity test if he still doubted that she was his daughter. Then, depending on Jonathan's response, they could decide on the next steps. Kato's wife suggested that Annie herself write a few words directly to him at the end of the letter, in spite of her poor writing ability, so that Jonathan had something directly from her as well. They hoped he would be moved enough to respond positively. It sounded like a good plan. Cesar could never have imagined that it was possible to love someone deeply without ever having met that person. Annie had shown him otherwise. He went home and wrote his first draft before he went to sleep.

He was surprised to get a voice mail from Annie the next day when he woke up, asking him to meet her for lunch. She apparently had some news for him. They met at a nearby *udon* (noodles) bar for lunch. Annie started off,

"I got all my immigration papers yesterday, and gave my boss two weeks' notice. I am on my way to the USA".

"Wonderful news! When do you leave? Where will you stay"?

"I will stay with my mother and stepfather in Las Vegas. So, I will check with them and then book my flight. Did you draft the email?".

"Yes", said Cesar, pulling out a copy,

"Here it is, but you should say something directly to him also."

Annie read the draft, liked it and added, *Dad, I go to live in Las Vegas with my mother in couple weeks. I am dying to meet you, and hope you want meet me too! Love you. Your daughter, Annie.*

"Cesar, I am so excited, cannot describe with right words in English. My life about to change in a few days. From Okinawa to Tokyo to Las Vegas! Little Annie is growing up, and will soon have a mother and a father! I wish you could come with me!"

"Yes, I feel the same way", he said, a bit lamely.

Cesar considered arranging a business trip to the US, and taking a few days off to visit Annie in Vegas. They went back to work after lunch, with Cesar promising to send the email off to Jonathan by the end of the day.

It was a difficult afternoon at work for Cesar. The volatile situation in the Middle East had put many investors assets at greater risk than they had been given to understand, and they were not happy. Cesar had to explain to his clients what some of their options were, and the pros and cons. He planned to finish the email that night, after visiting his favorite jazz club.

The jazz club was almost empty, with a few regulars including an older Japanese gentleman, bearded and wearing a black beret, whom Cesar recognized from past visits. In front of him was his *bottle-keep* which is a Japanese term and common bar practice for regular customers buying a bottle of liquor and having their name tags on the bottle. The bottle was kept at the bar, just for their consumption on future visits. It was a much less expensive option for regular customers than buying a few shots every time. Cesar had considered having his own bottle-keep of Oban at the club, but had not quite gotten there yet. He ordered his shot of Oban and sat back to enjoy the warmth of the single malt combined with the lilt of the smooth jazz.

There was a lot to think about. Cesar would have to remain involved. He wanted to date Annie but didn't even get a chance to fully express his feelings for her. Now she would be across the ocean, far away. She seemed to like him, but didn't want a relationship with him at a distance. Was something maybe possible if they visited each other often? Thinking more about it, Cesar realized that she could not get out of the US easily, so he would have to find a way to visit her often. Perhaps it would be too difficult anyway. Somehow the whiskey and the jazz combined to make Cesar philosophical and accepting of whatever fate had in store for him. *Flow with the tide*, let the tide of events take him over uncharted waters to unknown shores: a daughter, trying to reunite with her father, a woman whom he liked was going away, starting a new life in a far-away land. He could not date her because he was stuck in Japan while she, a Japanese, was emigrating to the States! Just a few days ago they were sitting side by side on a bench, on a warm August afternoon, on the tranquil grounds of the Meiji shrine. All very strange and unique experiences, merged into one heightened consciousness, with the warmth of whisky and the background of jazz, flowing with the tide.

Jonathan responded two days later to Cesar's email.
"My ex-girlfriend, Sayoko, did contact me many years ago to tell me that she was the mother of my daughter, but I did not believe her then. I am not sure I can believe you and Annie now. I have a wife and family, and my wife does not know anything about my relationship with Sayoko. I don't know what to think, or how to think. After Annie starts her life in the States, ask her to contact me again. My phone number is at the bottom of this email, but ask her to email me first. Bad English is OK. Japanese is OK too. I can get it translated. I am not promising anything, but we can go from there. I am sorry I cannot be more encouraging."

Cesar, however, felt it was fairly encouraging. At least Jonathan had responded, given his contact information, and had not given a flat refusal.

Jonathan had left the door open a little bit. When Cesar told Annie the next day, she had the same reaction as Cesar. Cautious optimism, mixed with excitement. After all these years, she had finally located him and he had responded to her. Her original plan was to start searching for him *after* going to the States, but Cesar's help had accelerated the search successfully! She told Cesar that she could not thank him enough and would always consider him to be one of her best friends, no matter what their relationship.

The next couple of weeks, Cesar hardly saw Annie. She was busy wrapping up her affairs in Tokyo, visiting her aunt and family in Okinawa, interfacing with her replacement at work, and doing the myriad things one has to take care of when permanently moving to another country. He was also very busy at work, and they decided to meet for lunch the day before her flight to the US. They went to the Okinawa restaurant again, a now familiar place. There was a table with two foreigners, a man and a woman and Annie, looking at them, whispered to Cesar,

"Look, a couple of Americans!"

"How do you know they are Americans? They could be Europeans or Australians or from any number of other countries?"

"No, no, look at how big and fat they are.", whispered Annie, with a conspiratorial smile. Cesar realized that she was probably correct in her guess. It was funny and sad at the same time. It matched his previous experiences in public places, and he could easily confirm it by listening to their conversation. The American English accent is distinctive with its nasal twang.

"Also, they have ice in their soft drinks. Americans always ask for ice".

Cesar hadn't realized that drinking soda with ice was so American, and made a mental note to check it out later. He told Annie that he may visit the States for work in a couple of months, and would definitely plan on meeting her then. Annie enthusiastically agreed. Lunch was over too quickly, and soon it was time for them to say good bye, much too soon. Annie would be leaving for the airport early the next morning, and she still had some last-minute stuff to take care of. She looked at him and said,

"I have a little gift for you".

She pulled out a music CD from her purse and gave it to Cesar.

"I like the music, so I thought of a present for you. Hope you enjoy it and think of me".

He thanked her. Then they hugged and went their ways.

Cesar gave her a couple of weeks to settle down, then decided to call her. Her mother picked up the phone and immediately said,

"I know who you are, Cesar, right?"

"Yes, Sayoko-san", replied Cesar, mindful of the honorific.

Annie was eager to talk to him. She had settled down, but had not actually called or communicated with her father yet. She said she had to be in the right frame of mind to do that, and it may take some time. Cesar understood. Annie was planning to enroll in a few courses during the upcoming fall semester at the University of Nevada, Las Vegas. One of them was English as a second language. She said she was happy and would send him some pictures of her life in Vegas. She was full of enthusiasm and it appeared that she was comfortable with Larry and Sayoko, although at one point during the conversation, she lowered her voice and said,

"I cannot talk much now".

He obviously could not ask her too many questions since she was not alone in the house. Cesar told her that he missed her. She laughed,

"Really? then come see me here!"

Cesar promised he would and would let her know when, but it should be within the next month or so. That night, as he lay in bed, Cesar had a vision of her in his mind: Annie in a red dress, wearing red lipstick, with the white umbrella over her head, a light rain falling, standing outside the Okinawa restaurant, looking at the taxis going by, waiting for him. It was a visual that seemed to be indelible, and he cherished it.

He kept on the lookout for a business trip to the US. Finally, the opportunity came when one of his clients wanted him to meet one of their senior board members at their headquarters in Houston. The meeting would be on a Thursday, so Cesar could take the Friday off, meet Annie on Friday and Saturday and take the late Saturday flight back to Japan. It would be tiring, but doable. He would get to see Annie after almost two months. He called Annie and told her the news. She seemed happy but not as enthusiastic as he had hoped she would be. He wondered if something was wrong. *Well, I will find out soon enough* he thought, as the day of his flight to Houston approached. On their next phone call, a few days later, Annie suggested that Cesar stay at a hotel in Las Vegas, where they would have privacy.

"Of course, I like you visit my family and meet Larry and Sayoko and my step-sisters, but it may be better if you stayed at hotel".

Cesar thought that was a good idea too, so he booked a room at the Bellagio on Las Vegas Boulevard for two nights, planning to arrive in Vegas from Houston on Thursday night. His trip was still over a week away, but he was feverish with anticipation. It was not just for meeting Annie, but he had become personally involved with her efforts to contact her father and he was eager to see that really happen. It was as if he was searching for his own relative. He would urge Annie to take the necessary steps as soon as possible. Cesar felt she should get back to Jonathan soon. A few weeks had gone by already. It wouldn't be prudent to wait too long. Cesar was known among his friends for having a great deal of empathy for people. In this case, he could feel and think like her at a deeper level than even he thought possible. Maybe it was because he liked her, and was close to being romantically attached to her.

The long-awaited day finally came when Cesar boarded the American Airlines flight at Tokyo's Narita airport. He was seated next to a Chinese lady who was returning home to Los Angeles after visiting her family in China. She had been living in California for over fifteen years but hardly spoke any English. The Chinese community in the Los Angeles area was so big that it was possible to survive well without having to learn English. It is a shame though, Cesar thought, not to pick up the language of the country you are living in for so many years! He had to spend more time on his Japanese.

He was able to nod off on the flight, but after arriving in Houston, after a two-hour layover at Los Angeles International, he was still very tired and jet lagged. His work the next day went well. In fact, there was the strong potential that a follow-on visit opportunity would come up a month later, and Cesar was quick to encourage that prospect with his clients. Then it was time for Vegas. The short flight seemed too long, as did the taxi ride from the airport to the hotel. Immediately upon checking in at the Bellagio, Cesar called Annie.

"Wow, what a beautiful lobby! My first time inside Bellagio. I have heard so much about it!", said Annie. They went up to his room on the twenty fourth floor. The view from his room was mostly the strip with dusty hills in the distance and a bit of the airport at one corner. Annie went straight to the window and took in the grandeur of Las Vegas, the man-made playground in the Nevada desert.

"How different this is from the Meiji shrine where we were together last time!"

Then suddenly she turned around,

"I haven't yet the courage to contact my father".

"You must do it quickly",

"Yes, yes! but can I wait another week? I need to picture myself writing to him. I have to put it all together in my head. Also, I was waiting to meet you".

Cesar told her that he may actually be back to the US for a follow up business trip the next month. He hoped that by then the contact with her father would have happened.

"Certainly, that is my plan".

Annie turned back again to look out the window. Cesar walked over to her and gently put his arm around her. Annie leaned a bit closer to him. Cesar could never bring himself to be aggressive in these situations. The situation with Annie was even more complicated because she had already told him clearly in Tokyo that she liked him but could not date him, and she gave him the reason for her decision. Nothing had really changed since then. Yet he had helped her with locating her father, and here they stood in his hotel room, close to each other, so near and yet so distant. After a while, Cesar stepped away, and the moment was gone.

They spent the next couple of hours roaming around the hotel and the casino area. They saw a few original Picasso's at the named restaurant, saw chocolates being made from scratch at a chocolate factory store, visited the famed Conservatory and Botanical Gardens and, soon after dark, enjoyed the iconic dancing water fountain show. When the show was over, Annie told him that she should soon be going back home.

"Cesar, what is the plan for tomorrow?"

"Why don't you come over late morning and we can plan then. I will think about it tonight".

She hopped on to a taxi, and Cesar went back to his room.

Cesar could not quite understand his own thoughts relative to Annie. Was she just a friend, a possible future dating opportunity, or both? Did he just feel protective about her because of her situation and vulnerability? Why did he like her? Was it just because he had gotten involved with her problems, or was there something intrinsic to her that was fundamentally attractive to him? Similarly, he wondered how she regarded him. Did she like him a lot, but was not willing to get emotionally involved because a relationship at a distance was fraught with problems? Or did she not like him much at all, and used the distance as an excuse? Was she even thinking about a relationship at this stage of her life? Was he just someone she was taking advantage of, in helping her contact her father? Was she even thinking beyond connecting with her father? He definitely liked her, and maybe tomorrow he could bring up the topic of relationship again. After all, it had been a while since that afternoon at the Meiji shrine when she had told him that she did not belong in Tokyo, but for the time being, he did! What an ironic juxtaposition!

The next day Cesar took Annie to several different casinos and an outlet mall. He bought her a dress she liked and they went to a show at the Bellagio in the late afternoon. Cesar had seen the same show years ago, but it was the first time for Annie to see any show in Vegas and she loved it. Cesar just could not bring up the topic of their relationship the whole day. He did urge her not to wait too long before contacting Jonathan. They talked a bit about her mother and Larry and her step sisters, and then Annie suddenly asked,

"Tell me something, would you mind if I started going out with someone here"?

The question surprised Cesar, but he was able to answer instantly,

"Of course not! I would be happy for you. Did you meet someone you like?"

"Not exactly yet, but there is a boy in my neighborhood who my mother knows. He is in one of the same classes as me. I think he likes me, and he is nice."

"Great, let me know if something develops!".

"Sure, you will be the first to know".

They stood waiting for a taxi at the lobby and when the taxi arrived, Annie suddenly held Cesar close, kissed him on the cheek, close to his lips, and said,

"You have been so nice to me, you mean so much to me, I really wish you well. I wish our situations were different!"

Then with a smile and a look, she was gone. Cesar did not know it then, but that would be the last time he would ever set eyes on Annie.

Cesar went back to his room. Overall, he felt good about the trip to Vegas. He realized that very likely Annie would start going out with someone soon. She was too attractive for guys not to go after her, and she could not and should not avoid the attention. She had a tough life and deserved to have a boyfriend and a normal relationship. Back in Tokyo, the next two weeks were a whirlwind of emergency situations at the office, so Cesar did not have much time to think about anything else except work. He confirmed with his Houston client that the next trip would be after almost exactly one month. He would call Annie and make plans to meet her once the actual dates were known. After a week, his boss told him that the date was confirmed and he could make plans for another trip to the US. He decided to call Annie the next morning from home, and give her the details of his upcoming visit.

He called Annie from his bed, and when she picked up, said
"Hi, I got some news for you!".
"Oh, your trip fixed?"
Cesar told her the dates he would be in Houston, and after Houston, Vegas, just like before.
"Great! but I have to give you some news too", said Annie.
Cesar's heart beat faster because he knew it must have to do with her contacting Jonathan.
"I emailed him and he emailed me back!"
"Really, wow! What did he say?"
"He said he will think about it some more and get back to me within a few days".
"Wonderful! Hope he agrees to meet you!"

There was a short silence at the other end of the line, and Cesar wondered what Annie was thinking. "Cesar, I have something else to tell you".

"OK, I am all ears".

There was a long silence, and this time Cesar knew it was about the guy who liked her. He knew that his relationship with Annie was over, before it ever began. Then Annie finally said in a low voice,

"I met someone I like".

Cesar heard himself instantly responding,

"Oh, great news! Is it the same guy you told me about? I am so very happy for you! Can you tell me more?"

There seemed to be a strange disconnect between his heart and mind and those words he had just spoken. This was not the first time in his life that a girl he liked, and hoped for a relationship with, told him that she liked someone else. His first reaction then also was to hide his true feelings, put on a brave front, and congratulate her. Annie was happy and effusive.

"He also Japanese American. His name is Ken, short for Kentaro. He is in my class at school. He born in Hawaii and grew up in Hawaii and Las Vegas. We just started going out a few days ago. I told him everything about you and how much you helped me. He very much wants to meet you. I am hoping that we can all get together at Larry and Sayoko's when you visit next month!"

"Of course, I want to meet him too", said Cesar, without much conviction.

They talked a few minutes more about her classes and then ended the conversation with Cesar giving her the details of his trip plans and promised to call her from the Bellagio Hotel upon arrival in Las Vegas, like last time.

After a busy day at work, with the thought of Annie and Ken at the back of his mind all day, Cesar decided he needed a stiff drink or two at the jazz club after a quick dinner. He was surprised at how quickly he was able to accept Annie's changed status. However, there was still a pain and deep sense of loss, mixed with a feeling of being happy for her, which he had told her about. The jazz club was not too busy. There was a guitarist playing classical jazz which suited Cesar's mood and he ordered a double Oban, and contemplated where he was in life. Annie was no longer available, that was a loss, but there was still Tokyo. Cesar liked Tokyo. It was a vibrant city. A city that the locals often did not fully appreciate the charm of, but foreigners more often did, because they could compare with other great metropolises. *Only if he could learn the language fast enough*, thought Cesar, the city would have much more to offer. He tried to imagine what Ken looked like. He was obviously younger than Cesar. He hoped he was mature enough for Annie, for Annie was certainly mature beyond her years. He hoped Ken would make Annie happy. She deserved it. His work was challenging, but going well. The Houston client had put in a good word for him, and his bosses were happy. This upcoming trip would be good from the work point of view, but painful from the Annie perspective. Cesar smiled to himself, let the warmth of the Oban take over, and realized that he had to *flow with the tide*, never knowing which way the tide will take him.

The days until his trip were hectic and thankfully passed quickly. After an uneventful flight to Houston and after finishing his work, Cesar called Annie just before leaving for Las Vegas. She didn't pick up or return the call, and Cesar thought that was odd. In any case, he would call her from the hotel and they would plan when and how he would meet with her family and Ken. After checking in at the Bellagio, he called her again. Again, she didn't answer and she had not tried to call him back either. This time he found it more than a bit odd, because she knew when he was expected to arrive at the hotel.

After a while he decided to call Larry and Sayoko's home number, which she had given him. This time a lady picked up.

"Who are you?"

Cesar knew from her accent that she was very likely Sayoko, Annie's mother.

"I am Cesar, a friend of Annie's. Can I speak with Annie, please?"

Cesar heard a distinct gasp at the other end and then just caught the beginning of a sob before the line went dead. His brain in a whirl, he called the number again. This time a different lady picked up.

"Are you Cesar, Annie's friend?"

"Yes".

"I am Joanne, Larry's sister", she said in a matter-of-fact voice.

"Sayoko asked me to talk to you. We all know about you. I am very sorry to have to tell you some very bad news".

Cesar sat down on his bed, unable to even ask what the bad news was.

"Annie and Ken were driving in the San Gabriel mountains near Los Angeles a few days ago, and he lost control of the car on a sharp curve, and …", her voice trailed off into a slight sob.

Cesar was numb with shock. Before the realization even sunk in that he would never see Annie again, he asked, "Did she ever meet her father?"

"No, but she got a positive reply from him and she was so very happy, she thanked you."

"The family is requesting that if you would like to contribute in her memory, please send your donation in her name to the Pearl Buck Foundation which supports and cares for marginalized children worldwide".

Cesar hung up, sat down on the bed and cried out loudly and uncontrollably like he hadn't cried ever before in his adult life. This was so meaningless, so unfair, so cruel! It seemed so unreal. Then dark thoughts crossed his mind. Could it be foul play? Did Larry take out life insurance on Annie? Could Larry have sabotaged the car Ken and Annie drove on their trip? How could anyone even dream of harming such a sweet and vulnerable girl? Futile thoughts! Cesar did not have the time or inclination to investigate. He had to just accept the accident and walk away. There was a faint hope in the back of his mind that it was all a mistake, or that it was an arranged disappearance, and Annie was still alive. He had floated with the tide, but now the tide had suddenly disappeared, leaving him in anguish, as on a dry beach on a hot summer day. He lay in bed all day, did not feel like eating anything, had a sandwich from the hotel room service, changed his flight to a day earlier than planned, and left for Tokyo the next day. He had hardly slept the night before. Annie's face with her intense eyes and enigmatic smile kept flashing in his head. She seemed more alive in his mind's eye than she had ever been in life. He planned to sleep on the flight back.

At the end of his assignment in Tokyo, Cesar returned to Manhattan. He did not seriously date anyone during the rest of his stay in Japan, although he had several opportunities to do so, and never went to either the Okinawa restaurant or the Meiji shrine again. A few months later there was a mysterious missed call from a restricted number on his mobile phone, and a tantalizing voice mail with just one word, "Hi", in a female voice that was difficult to pinpoint. Cesar hoped that would be Annie, but there was no second call, ever.

Years later, on a business trip to Tokyo, he went back to the Meiji shrine and walked up the same graveled path that he and Annie had treaded so many years ago. The majestic trees and the tranquil atmosphere had not changed, even the people seemed the same, although of course they were different. He walked to the end of the path, to the shrine itself, and looked at the board with the little plates of wood with wishes written on them. A pigeon startled him as it flew by. It was just as if yesterday that Annie and he had written their wishes and hung them there. He could almost feel her presence, standing by his side.

Her wish had indeed come true, such was the power of the shrine, the power of belief. He bought a plate and simply wrote, *May Annie's soul rest in peace* and hung it with the others. He looked at the plate for a long time and then walked back to the train station slowly. Annie may be gone, but her soul, her presence, seemed to be everywhere around him.

The magic of Annie's presence was dispelled as soon as he joined the human tide of commuters. He became just one of many, all going somewhere, all flowing with the tide.

ANOTHER WORLD

There are worlds within worlds – each with a fascinating story!

Brett Engler had lost a little over a quarter of a million dollars that day, but he took it in stride, and was happy that he could walk away from the poker game with a little over one hundred thousand left in his pocket. He could go home and focus on finishing the research paper he was working on. Tomorrow would be another day.

Brett parked his car in his parking spot under his four-story condominium complex, carefully checking his rear-view mirror for any unknown people that may be around. Although there was a security gate to the complex, and it was bright daylight, he could not be too careful, since he had a lot of cash and chips on him. The casino chips were the same as cash and convertible in the casino where Brett played poker. He had no time that day to follow his usual procedure of keeping the cash and chips in the safe deposit in the casino. One hundred and eight thousand dollars was a rather large sum to be carrying around in his backpack, but Brett was used to it. No one knew that he had the money on him and no one had followed him home. He was dressed inconspicuously in faded jeans, white t-shirt and a hoodie, and he felt safe. He took the elevator to the fourth floor. He had leased the condo a couple of years ago when he had moved from Mountain View, California to Las Vegas, and it had served him well. He had chosen the place for a combination of factors, chief among them being a gated complex, front door access privacy, low noise level during the day, availability of a gym, and a view. Reaching his door, he was about to insert his key into the lock when, out of the corner of his eye, he saw a man in gym clothes, with a towel around his shoulder, turn the corner of the hallway and walk rapidly in his direction. Although he had never seen the man before, the man appeared to know him and shouted "Hi, Brett!"

Brett was not too nervous, but he would take no chances. He quickly turned the key in the lock without fumbling, entered the condo in a flash and was able to close and lock the door just before the man knocked on it.

"Hey Brett, want to talk with you".

"Who are you, and what do you want?"

"I am on the third floor, directly under you. I am Drew Casey, a reporter for the Las Vegas Sun and I saw you on TV yesterday, playing a high stakes cash poker game. I barely know the basics of poker, having played in a few home games, but I admire you guys. Wondering if I could have a chat with you!"

"I have a phone call to make, Drew. How about you stop by in thirty minutes?"

"Sure, thing. Thanks Brett".

Brett heard the gradually fading sound of Drew's footsteps as he walked towards the elevators.

After carefully putting his cash and chips in his favorite hiding place deep inside the dirty laundry basket, Brett proceeded to call his friend Tony, in Los Angeles. Brett and Tony organized private high stakes poker games in various cities, where the players could win or lose hundreds of thousands of dollars in a few hours. These games were probably some of the highest stake games anywhere in the world. Most of the players were well heeled businessmen and bankers who played for fun and did not care about the money. Brett and Tony, and a couple of others, were the professionals or pros who spread these games and stood to win in the long run, but could also lose big on any particular day. In football, tennis, basketball or baseball, it is impossible to imagine a non-professional beat a professional even once. In poker, it happens every day, multiple times. It is only in the longer term that skill prevails in poker. The next game was being planned for the coming Friday evening at the high limit section of a well-known poker room in Vegas. Brett and Tony discussed how they would organize the game. Tony was supposed to round up the Russians Ivan and Danil, who played the previous week. Ivan was a pro, but his friend Danil was a real estate magnate who enjoyed the action of the game, win or lose. Tony would also call Spiro the banker from Houston who was spending the month in Vegas and confirm that he would play. Brett, for his part, would contact Mark, the Hedge fund owner, and Rita, the co-founder of the trust that controls one of the NFL's most well-known franchises. Together with Brett and Tony, that made the quorum of seven players. They may be able to add an eighth later if Henry, the Macau casino executive showed up in town. They discussed how to diplomatically reject the requests of a couple of other professional players who wanted to play. All high stakes games were privately organized although they were held in public cardrooms, and the organizers, like Tony and Brett, were careful to balance professionals and so-called recreational players for the betterment of the game and their personal opportunities. They also discussed an outstanding debt from one of the players who had requested a marker the previous week and had not yet settled his account. Brett and Tony both knew he was good for the debt and did not worry about it much. Business discussion over, Brett mentioned to Tony that a reporter who lived in the same condo complex wanted to chat with him right after the call. Tony warned him to be careful in not giving any reporter too much information about their games, and to respect the privacy of the participants. Brett agreed and they hung up. Brett still had about fifteen minutes before Drew was coming by, and he lay down on the couch to relax, with soft classical music from the local FM station playing in the background.

Brett, known as Dr. Engler or Professor Engler in academic circles, went by Brett, or BE in the poker world. Very few people knew his full name and only his closest friends knew his academic credentials. Born and raised in British Hong Kong, Brett was a brilliant student of Computer Science at the University of Hong Kong when China took over the former British colony in 1997. Brett's father, an Englishman, with an abundance of foresight, sent him to Cornell University in Ithaca, New York, to continue his undergraduate studies in Computer Science. Cornell had an exchange program with the University of Hong Kong, and it was not too difficult for a good student to manage a transfer. It was at Cornell that Brett learned the basics of poker, playing with his friends, and sometimes with his professors, at their homes, but his focus was on his studies. His parents, and specially his father, played various card games including bridge with friends at home. His father had tried without success to interest Brett in learning bridge. He never played poker, but listened to Brett's poker stories with interest.

Brett continued to excel at his coursework, and after his BS, continued directly on to the Ph.D. program in Computer Science at Cornell. He received his PhD in three years, and was offered an Assistant Professor job at New York University, which he eagerly accepted. His goal was to excel in research in the Machine Learning area of Artificial Intelligence and, within a couple of years, he was able to publish two key papers in the field that significantly enhanced his international reputation. Brett was able to develop a new algorithm that was able to predict human purchasing trends for luxury items, with a significantly higher hit rate. After three years, NYU offered him an Associate Professorship, which was a tenured position. That meant his future was secure in the academic world. Companies like Google and Amazon offered Brett attractive salaries to lure him away from his faculty position, but Brett was not interested in money *per se*. The intellectual challenge of furthering the frontiers of research was far more exciting. In his mid-30's, Brett was near the top of his field, with nowhere to go but further up.

During his years at Cornell and then at NYU he continued to play poker as a hobby and a passion, and found it challenging across many fronts. He knew his strengths and also his weaknesses. He deeply understood the math that underlies the decision-making process in poker, but he had not quite figured out how to blend in human psychology into the math and use that knowledge to make even better decisions. For Brett, research in Computer Science seemed easier than improving his poker game.

It was just after his promotion to Associate Professor that Brett received an offer of a one-year sabbatical to Stanford University at their world-famous Artificial Intelligence Laboratory (SAIL) that was to change his life forever in a way no one could have guessed. He accepted the offer, and soon after starting to work at SAIL, he discovered that the cardrooms in California offered poker in a public, easily accessible and open setting which was quite different from playing with friends at home. One could play anytime during the day or night and for however long one wished without any pressure to join, play on, or leave. The position at SAIL not only allowed Brett to delve into new areas of Artificial Intelligence, it also allowed him to discover new frontiers in poker.

During a Conference in San Jose, Brett visited one of the cardrooms where he was introduced to a group of players who played a type of poker called Limit Hold'em (LHE). Poker has dozens of variations and Texas Hold'em, as it is commonly known, is one of them. LHE is a type of Texas Hold'em where each bet is of a fixed pre-determined *limited* amount, hence the name. The most common version of Texas Hold'em is called No Limit Hold'em (NLHE), in which there is no maximum bet amount, and the player can vary his bet at any time by any amount. In NLHE, a player could bet all the chips he has in front of him, also known as 'All-In' at any time. Although the games appear to be similar, they require quite different strategies. The highest stakes games are, paradoxically, very often of the 'Limit' type. Brett had played LHE at Cornell and also in some home games in New York, but for relatively small stakes, where one could win or lose a maximum of a few hundred dollars during the course of an evening. The games at the cardroom which Brett visited in the Bay area were much bigger. Each pot (the amount of money that players were playing for on each hand) was several thousand dollars and a player could easily win or lose upwards of five to ten thousand dollars in a session.

Brett quickly learned not only how to become more proficient at LHE, but also enjoyed being part of the group of people who played the game regularly. Brett learned that although players appeared and disappeared over the course of months, years and decades, there were some who had been part of the scene almost forever, and these players provided a continuity of the culture of the game that combined tradition with the values and approaches of the younger players. What struck Brett was the diversity of the player population. Players ages ranged from the early twenties to mid-eighties. Their backgrounds were diverse, and their cities and countries of origin spanned the globe and all the States within the US. You were likely to find a Vietnamese who was one of the original 'boat people' sitting next to a lawyer, born into a privileged Massachusetts family, who owned one of the largest Corporate Law firms in California, or next to a Harvard trained neurologist or a venture capitalist. You were likely to find an Indian hedge fund manager sitting next to a retired Mexican roofing business owner or a senior executive at a blue-chip company, or a firefighter. On some days a reality TV participant or the owner of a restaurant chain would stop by to play. You were also likely to find a person who nobody knew anything about, looking like he had just gotten out of jail, sitting next to another such person who looked as if he may soon end up in jail. The common factor was that all of them were focused on the cards being played, sitting at the same table, enjoying the thrill which each new card brings, whether it be the thrill of victory or just the thrill of the experience.

A startling revelation for Brett came when he was well into his second month of regular play at the casino. One of the older players was friendly with Brett and he looked very much like one of Brett's professors in college. The aquiline nose, intelligent eyes behind black rimmed glasses, the scraggly beard, an impish smile, and quick wit, all were matching, although they were obviously different people. One day, while sitting next to him at the poker table, Brett decided to ask him what he did for a living, fully expecting to hear that he was a faculty member at some local college or university.

"This", said the man, with his characteristic impish smile, pointing at the table.

At first Brett did not get his meaning. After some clarification, he realized that the man played poker for a living. It was completely outside of Brett's life experience to comprehend that anyone could play cards for a living. However, a few more private conversations with the man opened Brett's eyes to a world where there was the opportunity to make the game into a business venture, where, just like in any other business, one makes a profit by using one's savvy to provide something of value to others. In this case, those making a living from poker use their knowledge and skills to provide entertainment to the so-called recreational players in exchange for an overall expectation of profit in the long run. For the first time, Brett was exposed to the concept of a professional poker player.

Brett got into this world of LHE players, determined to do well in the high stakes game. It wasn't easy, but before his sabbatical ended, through a combination of luck and skill, mostly skill, Brett had improved his game significantly. More than the money itself, for Brett, the real fun was to have a deep understanding of what was going on, develop a strategy based on that understanding, execute on the strategy, and see the results. During a session of poker, this cycle occurs hundreds of times, which contributes to the excitement of the game. On days he lost, he could attribute his losses to either luck or mistakes or a combination of both. Overall, he had won a significant amount of money by any standards and even after returning to New York at the end of his SAIL sabbatical, he visited the Bay area cardroom several times every year to continue playing the high stakes LHE game.

It was in the cardrooms in Southern California, however, that Brett suddenly broke through into the big leagues. The stakes were much higher, and the players were less skilled. Within the short span of a year Brett had amassed a bankroll worth almost two million dollars. The money was not really his to keep though. The higher the money available for playing, the less attractive the lower stakes games became, and the natural tendency was to play even higher. The danger was that the risk of loss, proportionately, was bigger and what was a depressing hundred dollar losing session in college would become a hundred thousand dollar, or even larger, loss. It required strength of mind and a firm belief that skill and statistics would ultimately prevail, to endure such losses.

Brett had studied the history of the game's big winners and losers over the decades and had detected and analyzed patterns that led to success or failure. That was his skill, to analyze patterns, establish hypotheses, draw conclusions and hone those conclusions by his own experience. Same as in the machine learning aspect of Artificial Intelligence. The difference was that, to do well in poker, to be a true professional, the player had to deal with and control his emotions. *Emotions*, in mathematical terms, meant anything that did not completely conform to logic or rational behavior. Statistics and the math of Game Theory always ruled supreme, rewarding or punishing emotional actions randomly and with total nonchalance. Brett knew that, and also knew that given the impossibility of completely controlling emotions, it was important to leverage emotions to gain information. Information regarding an opponent's hidden cards is the key to using statistics with leverage. Brett had figured out that although many players relied on game theory models to determine the correct plays, game theory and knowledge of statistics just by themselves did not adequately take into account the variations that can be caused by a player's emotions. Poker is a game that rewards the best decisions made by using the best judgment of people and mathematical probability with *incomplete information* on both those fronts.

It was in Southern California that Brett met Tony, also from Hong Kong originally. Tony was from a business background and came from a family of hoteliers. He took a liking to Brett, took him under his wing and offered to invite him to a super high-stakes game, also known colloquially as *nose-bleed stakes*. Brett still remembered the question Tony had asked him:

"Do you have a million that you can afford to lose?"

"Yes!", Brett had replied.

After playing in over a dozen sessions over six months, Brett, with the help of some luck, had built up his bankroll to a marginally comfortable seven million dollars. Marginally, because the swings in each of the nose-bleed games could be huge. Even if Brett was playing his best game, a couple of back-to-back losses could mean losing twenty-five to thirty percent of his bankroll, and that could be a trigger for loss of emotional control, and a further spiral downwards.

Although he had turned a significant profit, Brett was self-aware enough to realize that his driving motivation was the thrill of competition and coming out ahead, not the money itself. However, he had to balance that with a regard for holding on to the money he had earned, to avoid the risk of losing it all for the sake of competition. Such was the challenge of poker: the need to balance prudence with the competitive instinct, even when one has an edge over the competition.

The TV cash games, which his journalist neighbor Drew Casey had seen him playing in, were more for fun than profit. One of the players in Brett's regular high-stakes games knew the TV host of a poker show in which players played against each other with their own money, but received a handsome royalty from the TV streaming channel, which more than covered their initial buy-in to the games. Brett played in these games occasionally. The TV wins and losses were small, never nose-bleed.

There was a knock on the door. Brett had dozed off after his call with Tony, and at first wondered who could be knocking. Then, remembering that a Drew Casey from the Las Vegas Sun wanted to chat with him, he opened the door and let Drew in. Drew looked around the modestly appointed condo, walked to the dining table and sat down at Brett's behest.

"Beer?"

"No, thanks, just water is good".

Then they got down to business. Drew explained that he wanted to write an article for the newspaper that highlighted an interview with a successful high-stakes poker player. Brett was an ideal candidate because he was recently on TV and did not appear to be a stereotypical poker player, whatever that meant. Brett agreed to be interviewed, but told Drew that he wanted to review what Drew wrote, and have the opportunity to edit it before publication. Having agreed to all that, and establishing the ground rules, they started talking. After over two and a half hours, they were both tired and decided to call it a day.

Two days later, on Friday evening, Drew sent Brett a first draft of his proposed write up by email. It was in the form of an interview dialogue, in question-answer format. Brett was playing in the Friday game which he and Tony had organized when the email arrived. He was doing poorly six hours into the game, but he had roughly six more hours to catch up, and try to get even. By the time the session ended, he had made up some of his losses but still was down a fairly large number. Although it was frustrating and disappointing, after a good night's rest, he would be fine the next day, comfortable in the thought that he had played his 'A' game no matter which way the cards fell. It was Saturday afternoon by the time he got to Drew's email and started reading.

The introduction was glowing. Drew had portrayed Brett as a successful player and a rising star. He had mentioned his academic background, but Brett removed any reference to the actual Universities he had attended and details of his field of research. There was a summary of his poker career leading up to the televised cash game a few days ago. Then came the Question & Answer part. Brett read on:

Drew: You started out as a successful Computer Scientist working in Artificial Intelligence. Don't you feel conflicted now that you are spending so much time and energy playing poker? How do resolve that apparent conflict?

Brett: *Apparent* is the key word. There is no conflict, in my mind. Yes, it is a change in direction and focus, but I always did and am still doing what I like and enjoy. That has never changed. I still enjoy guiding my

Research students, and I enjoy my poker. When I feel I cannot do both well enough, I will not enjoy doing both either, and I will make a decision on way or another; however, I will always continue to do what I enjoy.

Drew: I suppose that decision is likely to be to quit academia?

Brett: Yes, likely, but not certainly. There is also a distinct possibility that years down the line I may give up playing poker.

Drew: That is interesting. What event may trigger your decision to give up playing poker? Losses that become unmanageable?

Brett: I don't think so. Although short term big losses can hurt, I know from experience that over a period of a year, I have a very high probability of coming out ahead. It is not the losses, but I may tire of the stress because of the mental acuity and alertness needed for the action, irrespective of whether the result is a loss or a win. Also, there is the boredom factor. If I am not learning anything new, not constantly improving, I may get bored and move on to other things.

Drew: You mentioned that playing in the LHE game at the South Bay card club was both fun and a learning experience for you. Can you say something about the *fun* aspect of that experience?

Brett: It was a very interesting group of players. Cast of characters, I should say. Many of them had played together for decades and knew a lot about each other. There was the social aspect of it, not just poker. The players knew each other so well that there were fights, rivalries, discussions, arguments, jokes, backstabbing, ridiculous wagers on weird topics, and also activities outside of poker, like fantasy football leagues, dining out, or golfing.

Drew: *Ridiculous wagers on weird topics* sounds interesting. Seems it is not directly related to poker. Can you give some examples for our readers?

Brett: The best example I can give you is a story that goes back many years, but people remember it vividly as if it were just yesterday. As you know, social interactions in any community are a microcosm of life. There are often rivalries between players who have known each other for years. One day there was an argument between a short, Asian player, Dick, and a tall middle eastern player, Rima. Dick was not getting anywhere in whatever argument they were having, and was getting visibly angry. Finally, in frustration, Dick suddenly bet Rima two thousand dollars that his 'dick' (no pun intended) was bigger than Rima's. There was silence at the table, and then laughter. Neither Dick nor Rima was laughing, though, as Rima considered the proposition. The players did not really expect Rima to accept, so that when Rima actually accepted, the table was suddenly very quiet. This was something the likes of which no one had heard of or seen in their lifetime. In all proposition bets, the parties have to agree on details of the conditions that must be met for the wager to be settled. Over the next hour or so Dick and Rima discussed details of how they would measure the sizes, where they would do it, who would go first, what additional props they may use, and time constraints. After they reached agreement, they both left the table, and walked out together. The players at the table were left to reflect on the amazing proposition that they had just heard, which was being played out in real time, and speculated on who would win. Needless to say, there were all types of risqué comments and jokes, all quite appropriate to the situation. There were side bets between some of the players on who would win between Dick and Rima.

Drew: That is indeed an amazing wager. Do you know what agreements they had for settling the wager?

Brett: Yes, this is what I have been told by people who were there during their discussion of the conditions. The long and short of it (no pun intended) is that Rima and Dick would sit side by side in one of their cars in an isolated section of the huge parking lot of the casino. Then Rima would go first and use a ruler for the measurement. Dick would follow. They could not use any props except their hands, of course, to get to their best possible measurement. Since there would be no neutral third party, they would have a gentleman's agreement on who won, and the loser would pay the winner two thousand dollars cash. They would openly announce the winner in front of other players at the table after their return to civilization!

Drew: I can hardly believe what I am hearing. What happened next?

Brett: The players waited anxiously. A half hour passed, then an hour, and still no sign of the penile combatants. Finally, Dick showed up with a huge grin on his face.

Some thought he had won, but his first words were,

"Damn, it was hard".

There were loud guffaws.

"I mean it wasn't easy, and I lost, but I am sure anyone here would lose to Rima. Also, I am confident that if I take on anyone else here, I would win. I just bet against the wrong guy"!

The players nodded, some laughed. Those who had sided with Rima collected their side bet wagers. It was clear that Dick was trying to salvage some self-respect after losing, but no one challenged him any further.

Drew: Did anyone ask Dick or Rima details of what happened during their competition? (laughing)

Brett: They didn't have to ask. Dick had several amusing anecdotes. Apparently, it was not easy to sit next to each other in the close confines of a car in broad daylight in a public parking lot and try to get to the right timing for measurement. When Rima, who went first, was on the verge of achieving some level of success, they were surprised by an elderly lady walking by. That set them back at least fifteen minutes. Then Rima finally got to where he wanted to be. It seems that upon seeing what he had to compete against, Dick surrendered without even trying. He knew when he couldn't possibly measure up. It was possible, the players speculated, that Dick couldn't even get going knowing what he was up against. He conceded and paid up. That was the end of the story.

Drew: Did people talk about this incident later? Was there a sequel that may be of interest to our readers?

Brett: Not really, it seems that Dick basically self-destructed after that incident. He tried another bet against an opponent, a tall guy whom he often had arguments with, and he was sure to lose against. The story goes that he plunked down ten thousand dollars on the table and offered the same wager, but the contest never took place. Apparently, they could not agree on the conditions. Dick used the non-wager to save face. They talked about the Dick-Rima incident for years, and it was always good for a laugh. Not unexpectedly, Dick slowly withdrew from the community, fed up with the laughs, I guess! Rumor had it that he faced family as well as health problems and he finally stopped playing completely and disappeared.

Drew: That is indeed a good wager story. Any others?

Brett: One more interesting story comes to mind. One of the regular players was a fan of English poetry, and would always look forward to discussing poetry with anyone with similar interests. The problem was that very few people, at least in the poker world, had similar interests.

One day, quite accidentally, while chatting with a young man from the East coast, they discovered a common interest in poetry and more specifically in the poetry of Edgar Allan Poe, and even more specifically in Poe's classic poem, *The Raven*, probably the most famous long poem in American literature. Both of them apparently could recite large sections of the poem from memory, and as their competitive nature would have it, the conversation soon turned to whether they could recite the whole poem without making any mistakes. Keep in mind that 'The Raven' is one of the longest poems in American literature, and filled with difficult words. The next step obviously was the wager. The young man had two weeks to brush up, study and memorize the poem. Then he would have to recite it with three or fewer mistakes to win the wager of two hundred dollars. If he had four or more mistakes, he would lose. Poker players wager on many different things, but this was a first, like the other one I just finished telling you about. No one had ever heard of a poetry recital wager. The day of reckoning came, and the two of them sat at a table with a recorder and off they went. The young man put up a very creditworthy performance but lost the bet. He made four errors, just one over the 'line'.

Drew: A great story. Two quite different bets, on opposite ends of the spectrum, if I may say so.

Brett: Yes, I could tell you of various other bets, like who could hop farthest on one leg, or run a mile backwards, or write down all fifty states' names in less than three minutes, or jump higher to touch a TV on the wall or the top of a door frame, but the two I just told you are good examples for your readers, I hope.

Drew: (Laughing). Yes, agreed. I would now like to ask you some questions about the game of poker itself. We just talked about some of the social (and fun) aspects of the game. Do you get fun out of playing the game itself? Or is it purely for profit?

Brett: Anything that is challenging is also fun. Let me describe one hand of poker in a way that perhaps your readers will appreciate. This pretty much applies to every hand of LHE *anyone plays anywhere*. Sitting at a table, with seven or eight other players, everyone is dealt two cards face down from a randomly shuffled deck. It is the famous *hand you are dealt*. There are several rounds of betting, with more community cards coming into play. First three more and then one and finally one last card. By *community* cards I mean these cards are open and everyone can see them and use them for his hand. They are shared by all. There is anticipation and excitement as each card is revealed. There is the element of surprise, of knowledge-based analysis, involving both mathematical knowledge and psychology, and there is the joy or the agony of the final determination of win or loss. There are between ten to twenty decisions to be made during each hand, and then the whole thing is over in around two to three minutes. You hope that your decisions are better than that of the others. For the experienced player, the correct decisions are more important. For others, the win or loss on a hand is more important. Each hand is special and unique. Never before and never again, will a group of players get the same cards in the same order and be faced with the same decisions as what just happened. If you win, you have to be humble, if you lose you have to learn not to get angry or show your frustration, just move on to the next hand and another unique event will unfold. It is a constant adrenaline rush. Three minutes packed with so much punch. That is the fun and excitement of the game.

Drew: If better players always or mostly win, how can the game survive? Why would players who lose come back to lose more and more?

Brett: This is a topic that is not discussed openly in much detail in the poker world, for two reasons. First, although the weaker player loses in the long run, he actually can win in the short term, and comes to believe that winning or losing depends more on luck than skill. Second, the better players know who the weaker players are, but no one talks about it, except by innuendo, because it is an obviously sensitive topic. The weaker players win often enough to enjoy coming back. They do not have the long-term perspective. You cannot think of any other sport where an amateur can take on a world class player and actually beat him, or where a weak player does not realize he is weak. Poker is unique in this regard, and the lines between amateur and professional are a bit blurred in terms of immediate results. The amateur can share the fun, the excitement and the joy of winning almost as much as the professional. Conversely, the professional often experiences the pain of losing, just the same as anyone else. Such is the nature of the game.

Drew: You have lived a double life in a sense, an academic as well as a card player. Isn't there a stigma associated with the casino world, in the minds of people who don't know the difference between poker and other forms of gambling?

Brett: Yes, and I have to learn to live with it, deal with it, and oftentimes hide it. To most people, playing cards with money is gambling. It is only recently, with TV coverage of poker tournaments, that people have slowly begun to realize that there is skill involved in poker. Even so, I avoid talking about my card playing around my students or peers. It is only when I feel that the people who I am talking to are aware of the difference between gambling and poker that I feel comfortable talking about poker. The general social stigma is always there, though. When I take Uber from the airport to the casino, the driver often asks me if I like to gamble. I say "No", to which I get the frequent response,

"Then why are you going to the casino? To meet someone?".

I often say "No, I play poker".

Then he either knows that poker is not gambling, or asks me again and I explain to him the difference.

It was only after several years of constant discussion and explanations that my father began to accept my poker playing ventures. My mother still doesn't. Neither I nor my parents ever mention it to any other relative of mine. They would never understand and always would think of me as a lost, if not depraved, soul. I do not think that the perception and identification of poker with gambling will ever go away. As we discussed before, even among poker players, a majority of players do not think of poker as a game of skill. How can you expect non poker players to accept it as such?

By the way, another view I have often heard expressed is that even if poker is a game of skill and not really gambling, it is not a morally correct way to make money because you win money from individual players, taking advantage of their weaknesses, and possibly hurting their financial well-being in the long run.

Drew: How do you respond to that criticism?

Brett: I consider poker as a business, my business. Just like any other business, there is money exchanged for a product, and there is competition for that money. The product here is the game itself, the act of playing.

The competition is between all the players. Just as in any other business, strategy, skill, the ability to withstand adversity and the ability to learn from mistakes and improve, are all vitally important. Everyone who sits down to play knows upfront that he may win or lose. There is complete transparency. If there is a moral connection to be made, all businesses would come under scrutiny. Often the stated goal of business is to drive competitors out of the market. In poker, it is striking that winners and losers play together with a much higher level of camaraderie than in any other business or sport. In this case, as in many others, the morality card (pun intended) is played by those who don't know what they are talking about.

Drew: Let us talk about your super high-stakes games, which I have heard you play these days. How high are the stakes? Why are these stakes called *nose-bleed*? Who are the players? How are the games organized? How much do people in these games win or lose?

Brett: I have to be very careful what I tell you, Drew. Obviously, it is a very small world, the people are often well-known public figures and there is an implicit understanding in the community that nothing is more important than privacy. Most of the players would be more upset at outsiders learning about their losses (or wins) than the losses themselves. Still, I can provide some general insights for your readers.

The term *nose-bleed* began to be used during the heyday of online poker over twenty years ago. At high altitude, in the rarefied atmosphere, nose-bleeds are more likely to happen. Since the stakes in these games are super high, the term *nose-bleed* began to be applied to these games.

There is no hard boundary between high stakes and super high stakes. In the highest games I play in, the average win/loss is around three to five hundred thousand dollars. That means that the maximum win or loss in a particular session could very well be a million dollars or more. What I just told you also defines the player set. The players are from many different walks of life, with three key things in common between them: extreme wealth, extreme interest in the game of poker, and an ability to take big losses in stride. Without all three of these elements being present they would not be regular players. A friend and I organize these games usually once in two weeks, depending on player schedules and availability. They are usually held in a private room in some well-known casino, either in

Las Vegas or in the Los Angeles area, and sometimes in the East Coast, in Florida or New York.

Drew: Why play in a casino? These are private games. Why not have them in someone's home? Isn't that more private?

Brett: The game of poker has changed a lot since the days of the wild west, and also since Texas Hold'em first started about a hundred years ago. In those days, poker was a game which was played in saloons or people's homes. They were controlled by a few, and the weak were taken advantage of. The organizers and players brought guns to the games. Security was provided by individuals not organizations, and the focus was on exploitation. These days, with a much more regulated and controlled setting, it has become a combination of entertainment and business.

The infrastructure offered by a casino is very difficult to duplicate elsewhere. Security is one of the most important requirements of any poker game, and the level of security needed for a high stakes game is quite rigorous. There is very little crime inside casinos although you will not find such a large accumulation of loose cash in a public space anywhere else in the world. Cameras are ubiquitous and are a strong deterrent. Also, most games are played with chips instead of cash. The chips can be exchanged for cash at the casino cashier. This is related to security and also transactional convenience. For example, players often keep the chips without cashing them in, for use on another day. Another reason is the easy availability of services like food, drink, masseurs, clean restrooms, convenience stores, etc. When players play long hours, they need the extras which are not that easy to arrange in a private residence or in a hotel room. I have played in hotel rooms with good security, but it gets claustrophobic after several hours, and it is not easy to get something from outside or even to just take a walk, or for smokers to smoke.

Drew: How do you keep out players you don't know from your game? A casino is public space, is it not?

Brett: This is an issue we have to deal with every session, but not in the way you are thinking. The stakes are high enough that it is pretty near impossible for a random unknown player to just sit down and plunk half-a-million dollars cash on the table and ask to be dealt in. If and when that happens, we actually welcome it as long as the unknown player actually has the cash to play, because an unknown player is usually not a player to be afraid of. The problem is more with well-known professional players who would like to play and have a chance to win big money against weaker players. We have to manage the invitee list carefully, and to do so, we have to reject many requests from well-known players.

Drew: We have talked about normal stakes public games and nosebleed stakes private games. How about the TV games, like the one I saw you play in a couple of days ago?

Brett: TV cash poker games which are live streamed have become popular with a relatively niche viewing audience over the years. They usually feature well known poker faces and celebrities. The stakes are nowhere near as high as in the highest private games, but high enough to bring gasps from viewers who are not used to seeing players risk upwards of a hundred grand on the fall of a single card. Although the players are officially playing with their own money, they are very often subsidized by either the TV channel or by patrons who have a vested interest in the outcome. The cards can be seen by a tiny camera set at the edge of the table, and TV audiences can follow the action as it develops. Tournament poker first popularized these tables equipped with a live camera.

Still, in my opinion, as a spectator sport, poker lags well behind other sports. The reason is that *most of the action is in the player's head*. The actual motion of putting chips into the pot is the final result of that thought process which we cannot see. The best we can do is think what we would do in a similar situation and compare our hypothetical action with the TV player's action.

Drew: I am glad you mentioned Tournament poker. Do you play in them? What are the differences between Tournaments and cash games?

Brett: Tournaments are a structured system where the stakes go up as the play progresses, and you cannot buy more chips beyond a pre-set time interval after the start of the tournament. Everyone puts in money upfront into what is known as a prize pool and at the end, the money is distributed to the top twenty percent of the field, with higher places getting more. If there are a large number of entries, like in the Final event of the World Series of Poker Tournament held every year, it is possible for the top place finishers to make several hundred times their investment. I do not play tournaments often because I believe there is more luck involved in getting to be among the high finishers, and it takes a lot of time, often with no substantial return on investment. I am more comfortable with my chances in cash games. Having said that, I must add that I have done fairly well over the last several years in the final event of the World Series of Poker, which is held every year in Las Vegas. I made a little money, around fifty to sixty thousand, but I was far from the first-place prize which is usually six to eight million dollars.

Drew: We have talked a bit about how you balance your academic and poker related activities. Let's go a bit deeper into that. If there is a challenging research project with one of your students, with a deadline involved, that conflicts with a major poker game you are setting up or already set up, how do you handle that conflict – both mentally and practically?

Brett: That is an easy one. Poker will not get hurt by waiting. The game may be delayed, or postponed, but it will happen sooner or later. The players will be there, and new opportunities and schedules can be arranged. Academic research, on the other hand is time-sensitive. An idea must be worked on quickly, or the flash of inspiration may disappear. Does that answer your question, Drew?

Drew: Yes, it does. Let me ask you another question. One often hears about cheating in poker. Can you comment on the prevalence of cheating in the games you play and how you can control or monitor it?

Brett: It is a law of nature that whenever there are rules that are to be followed, there are people who will try to bend or break those rules to their advantage. This has been true of all human endeavors throughout the history of civilization. It has also always been the case that controls are in place to detect these deviations and correct or punish those involved. Finally, throughout history there has always been a fight for ascendancy between the cheater and the 'police'. If the police use one tactic or technology to catch the cheaters, the cheaters will use a different tactic or higher level of technology to evade the police. So, it is like the police and the cheaters climbing endless ladders with each one trying to be on a higher rung. This battle is constantly being fought in many different arenas, and poker is no exception. Poker has had its cheating scandals, and the policing has become stricter, but compared to many other fields of competition that I am aware of, it is surprising how few and far between the incidences of cheating are. In my experience, and to the best of my knowledge, there has been only one or two incidences where someone tried to cheat in a low stakes game in a casino. He was caught fairly quickly by players who knew that his actions were unusual, and he was barred from ever playing again. Of course, in online poker, where monitoring and controls are much more difficult to implement, there have been many more cases of cheating. Live poker, among people who know each other, works on a very strict honor system. Being caught doing something even slightly unethical can have far reaching effects. Losing the respect of your peers is worse than losing money.

Drew: You mentioned earlier that most people, including a majority of poker players think of poker as gambling rather than a game of skill. Gamblers are usually superstitious. Do you see superstition playing a role in the behavior of poker players?

Brett: Very much so. Superstition, after all, is nothing but assuming a correlation or relationship between actions and their outcomes, where none actually exist. For example, sometimes players would ask for a change of playing cards or they change their seats, thinking that the unlucky deck of cards or the unlucky seat caused their losses. There are much more extreme and somewhat funny examples of superstition-based actions. I can tell you some, if you are interested.

Drew: Sure, go ahead.

Brett: Sometimes a player will win and then wear the same clothes the next day, and if he did well again, wear the same clothes again. Other players may notice this and make fun of him. I remember one instance when players gave a gift of a cologne to someone who hadn't changed his clothes in three days.

There are examples where a player would go outside to the parking lot and change the location where his car is parked. The common feature in all superstition is that when people think they are unlucky for an extended period of time, they want to change something and hope that their luck will change for the better. Conversely, if a superstitious person is lucky, he is *afraid to change anything*. Superstitions are often culture dependent. Asian people consider it bad luck if someone touches their shoulder. Indians wear rings made of special gemstones and wear threads of different colors on their wrists to ward off evil spirits and bring good fortune. Some cultures think that rubbing the belly of a statue of the Buddha will bring them luck. There are all sorts of superstitions around any card game where odds and statistics play a key role. By its very nature, statistics underlies superstition and appears to justify it.

Drew: That is an interesting comment. What do you mean by *statistics underlies superstition and appears to justify it?*

Brett: Let us say that a player will win if he gets a card of a particular suit, say spades. The probability of that happening is, say twenty percent. The player says a little mumbo jumbo prayer and, lo and behold, gets a spade. If he is the superstitious type, he immediately associates the prayer with getting the card he wanted. He doesn't realize that if the same situation were to be played out a thousand times, he would get a spade two hundred times roughly and a non-spade card roughly eight hundred times, *whether he says his little prayer or not*. So, this time was just one of those two hundred times out of a thousand that statistics says he will get a spade, but our superstitious friend associates it with the prayer, because he doesn't realize that he is entitled to a spade by the laws of probability. Another situation that occurs quite often is that a player is unlucky for a long time, then changes something and gets lucky shortly thereafter. He associates the change he made with the change in luck. From a statistics standpoint, his luck would have turned for the better anyway, whether he made the change or not. Statistics appears to justify superstition. By the way, belief in luck lies at the basis of gambling. There would be no gambling without this belief in luck. Statistics decides what actually happens. Luck is how winners and losers describe it. Most poker players believe in luck and think that they can change it by falsely correlating it with some other action, like changing the deck of cards.

Drew: We have covered many different aspects of a poker players life and environment. Do you have any pointers for budding poker players that will help them improve their game? And any pointers for advanced players that you may care to share, although I understand if you choose not to.

Brett: For newer players, I would say: don't just think about your hand and your opponent's hand, also think about what your opponent thinks your hand is, and play accordingly. This is known as next level thinking.

Also, I would say, on some days just walk away – there will be another day! It is tougher to give advice to advanced players, but let me stick my neck out and try anyway. To advanced players, I would say: Try to observe and understand the overall style of play of your opponents, and then make use of that knowledge for your benefit. Very often we play against the same players day in and day out. Each player has a unique style. Try to figure out what your opponents are doing in different situations and how frequently they are doing it. Sometimes we are playing against a new opponent for the first time. In that case, try to quickly assess, even if very roughly, what type of player he is, and what are the meanings of his various actions. At the same time, reverse the thinking and try to picture how your opponent is thinking about your style, if he is thinking at all!

Poker is a game of best decisions with incomplete information. The degree of incompleteness can be somewhat in your control, though. So, for beginners, think about your opponent's perspective and have fun. For advanced players think about the opponent's overall style and continue to have fun! For non-poker players, watch the fun!

Drew: Well, Brett, thank you very much for your time and I am sure our readers will enjoy your insights.

Brett: Thanks for the opportunity to share my thoughts. Say *Hi!* to your readers and *good luck at the tables*, or should I say *good analysis at the tables*!

The article appeared two days later, and Drew sent a *Thank you* email to Brett after it appeared, and also mailed him a couple of copies of the newspaper. Brett sent a copy to his dad who had moved back to London from Hong Kong. He was happy to hear back from his dad that he got a better insight into the world of poker from the article, than he had before. He gave Drew credit for the conversational style of the article, which made it possible for Brett to express himself better.

Drew did not hear from Brett for a long time after that meeting and neither did he see him again on the TV poker shows. He often wondered whether Brett was continuing his high-flying ways or what he was up to. It was almost two and a half years later that Drew was flying back to Las

Vegas from San Francisco where he was visiting family, when he ran into Brett at San Fransisco airport.

Brett was hardly recognizable in a suit and tie instead of the poker players uniform of jeans or shorts, a tee shirt, sneakers, a hat and a backpack, which Drew was familiar with.

"Brett, remember me? I am Drew Casey, Las Vegas! How are you? What have you been up to? What's with the suit and tie, man?"

"Drew! Of course, I remember you. Yes, it's been a while, and there have been changes in my life. I have some time before my flight to New York and I can fill you in, on condition that this is not for an article in your paper".

"Go ahead, I am really curious, and I promise not to write about it.", said Drew.

Brett told Drew that he had continued to play high stakes poker for almost a year after the newspaper article. There were ups and downs and he began to question whether he was being challenged enough. He was making good money, and the game always had new challenges and twists that kept Brett's interests alive, but the new challenges were not novel enough. He was beginning to get bored with the repetitiveness of his lifestyle. He had met a woman shortly after his last meeting with Drew, and they had hit it off. She had moved in with him and was a great support to his poker as well as academic lifestyle. For the first time in his life Drew had someone else to care about, and this person cared about him.

Fortunately for Brett, he had kept up with his academic responsibilities and was well regarded at NYU for his support of his students' research. Suddenly a new opportunity had arisen. New York University had received a large grant for work on AI models to predict two quite different and unrelated natural phenomena: global climate changes and earthquakes. They offered to promote Brett to Full Professor and Director of a new Institute for the Global Applications of Artificial Intelligence. He would have his choice of research students and control the funds and direction of research. Also, NYU would share resources in this project with Columbia University allowing Brett to oversee several Associate and Assistant Professors as well as graduate students at both universities. Brett had decided to find out more details of the projects before committing himself and had spent three months studying the opportunity in more detail. He liked what he saw and decided to accept the offer.

"It was a no-brainer for me. Few get the opportunity to be involved in a project that has the potential to benefit humanity, not just today but for all time to come. There is no risk of success or failure; just being involved and contributing in whatever way I can, is success. Poker has taught me a lot about life. It has also taught me to respect the world outside of poker. I will never forget poker and will still play when the opportunity becomes available, just not professionally. I have to listen to a higher voice - I have to move on. I accepted my new role a year ago, and am returning home from a conference in San Fransisco. My woman is waiting for me at home, and I am happy I still have most of my poker winnings saved up for a rainy day."

Brett paused, then continued,

"However, don't count me out yet. Sometime down the line, in some game, somewhere, you may still hear me utter the timeless words for a poker player: *Deal me in*!"

Brett finished talking, got up and said he had to go. Drew had been listening quietly, and could not think of much to say. He shook Brett's hand, hugged him and wished him well in his new venture and new life. *It would be good, if we could really predict earthquakes and figure out how to deal with climate change*, thought Drew.

As Brett walked towards his boarding gate, he looked inside a bar and saw a TV poker show being live-streamed. Without a second look he kept walking, walking towards his new and exciting life.

NEVER ALONE

Alternate realities are also real

"Dad, I am *never alone*. They are always talking to me. I just wish I could, even for one day, be like my old self, be just by myself". Ajay could not offer any advice, consolation, or a solution. He knew that those words defined his son, and he also knew that his relationship with his son had changed forever.

Ajay often stopped by the deli at Union Square whenever his work took him to San Francisco. The eclectic Italian deli made panini just the way he liked, and that, together with a glass of wine, was usually enough fortification for people-watching which he enjoyed. He was an active people watcher. Not willing to just gaze lazily at those passing by, he would try to figure out where they were from, try to read their faces and imagine their lives and backgrounds. When it was a couple or a family or a group, he would let his mind dwell on their possible relationships. He might read more into a smile or a frown or a gait than there was possibly there, but the exercise was always fun. Tourists made up a large proportion of the people walking by and Ajay would try to guess which countries they were from, by their appearance, dress, or recognizing a word here or an accent there. He could always let his mind wander on to something else, and the people would provide just a kaleidoscopic background. People watching was an art, practiced by many but practiced well by few.

Striking up a conversation with a stranger was a totally different ball game. That required boldness, focus, commitment, and a sense of adventure. It was not for the self-conscious, the timid or the risk-averse. Ajay was not particularly good at it, although he had undergone training as a door-to-door salesman in his college years, and been quite successful in that enterprise over a couple of summers. At the end of his work day, he usually sat by himself, accompanied by his glass of wine and a sandwich, watching people, thinking about this and that, and often about his children. Lately, he had often felt the urge to go to one of the many bars around town and talk to someone, anyone, about his life and the situations he was dealing with, and get things off his chest, but that was easier said than done. Although he had been facing an extremely challenging situation with his son for an extended period of time, he felt that very few people he knew could have done much better in dealing with his situation. He had a practical philosophy of life which allowed him to tread the middle ground between extremes of emotions. He knew that people could be lucky or unlucky, but in the final analysis everything was statistical. A certain percentage of humanity would enjoy or suffer in a particular category, be lucky or unlucky. If not him, it would be someone else, but for all people, over all of time, the laws of statistics prevailed - there was no luck in the equation. This realization helped Ajay deal calmly with situations that would have felled most people.

That day, Ajay had finished work a bit earlier than usual, and decided to grab a late lunch at the deli, planning to do some shopping at Macy's afterwards before heading home. It was a beautiful late fall day in San Francisco, a bit cold but not too windy, with a few scattered clouds in a clear blue sky. A streak of sunlight fell on the iconic Westin St. Francis Hotel, giving the hotel and its immediate neighborhood a roseate glow, which added to the charm of the Square. Most of the tables outside the deli were occupied, but he found one that was available and sat down with his panini and a glass of cabernet. Ajay enjoyed his cabernet. The bolder the better. Not for him the fruity reds which many of his friends liked and definitely not any white wine, with the exception of a few dry chardonnays which he would indulge in, only when no good cabernet was available. White wine tended to give him a hangover which, for some reason, red wine never gave him. Ajay was half way through his panini when he suddenly realized that a middle-aged lady was standing close to his table and trying to get his attention.

"May I join you? All tables are occupied around here."

She looked friendly and Ajay felt comfortable.

"Sure, please sit down. Ajay here".

"I am Rebecca, you can call me Becky".

Rebecca had also ordered a panini, and was waiting for it to be brought out.

"Where are you from, Ajay?"

"Originally from India, but I have lived here most of my life. I used to be in the technology sector, but I am retired and run my own small business now".

"How interesting!" said Rebecca politely, not really caring whether the stranger ran his own business or not. Her panini and coffee came and they were both busy eating for a while. It was lunchtime, on a weekday, and Union Square was filled with its usual mix of people. The office goers were dressed well, and walked with a measured gait without looking around. The tourists, casually dressed, carrying their water bottles, walked slowly, taking pictures with their smartphones, looking around, walking in erratic zigzags. Some were reading the inscription on the Dewey monument or staring at the buildings around Union Square. Some were just sitting on the steps around the square, looking at other tourists passing by. Then there were the hawkers who were peddling something or the other, approaching the tourists and mostly being waved away, but persisting with their offerings.

"I love watching people. There is a story behind every face." Ajay said suddenly.

This resonated strongly with Rebecca.

"I enjoy watching people too, and I try to figure out where they are from!"

Then they were both quiet for a while, as if following a cue to watch people together, now that they shared this bond. Several seagulls flew by overhead. The seagulls were watching people too, from their elevated perspective. A little girl shrieked with joy as one of the seagulls swooped close to her. Union Square projected the normal life of a vibrant city.

Ajay and Rebecca sat, not facing each other, but looking in the general direction of the quadrangle. All of a sudden, there was a distraction, if you could call it that. One of the many homeless people, who are often on the streets of San Francisco, was walking slowly towards them. He was dark skinned, wore a black hat and sunglasses, and was unkempt and unshaven. He was wearing several layers of clothing, all of which were dirty, as were his tattered jeans. He had a bulging backpack which was partly unzipped and a small American flag could be seen poking out of it. His gait was unsteady, swaying a bit, and he was talking to no one in particular, shaking his head from time to time, laughing at times, and sometimes waving his arms, as if in animated conversation. They watched him shuffle slowly by. He did not fit in with the crowd and yet, in a strange way he seemed an integral part of the Union Square scene. The immense diversity of San Francisco, Rebecca was thinking, included not only supporters of Donald Trump, or the followers of Elon Musk, but the homeless also. As he passed Ajay and Rebecca's table, he said something unintelligible in their general direction, laughed to himself and kept walking without waiting for any response from them. Although most of the other lunch customers studiously avoided looking at the man, Rebecca noticed that Ajay was staring intently at him, and watched him as long as he could, before he disappeared from view. Rebecca broke the silence first:

"There are so many of them on the streets these days, such a sad situation. I wonder what he is saying to himself".

Ajay turned his chair towards hers, and looked at her in the eye,

"Becky, let me tell you something, that man was not really talking to himself, although it appears so, and I can understand your thinking that way!"

"Who was he talking with, then?"

"He was carrying on a conversation with voices he was hearing in his head. It is one of the classic symptoms of schizophrenia".

Rebecca was silent for a while, trying to absorb what Ajay had just told her.

"Is there any treatment for schizophrenia?"

"It is a sad Catch-22 situation in many different ways. Mental illness is different from other illnesses in that the brain itself is affected, so the person does not recognize that he is ill. There is no cure, but although there are medications that can keep the symptoms under control, it is difficult to make an adult person take the medication on a regular basis, because he does not accept that he needs it. Even if he goes to a psychiatrist, gets diagnosed, starts treatment and gets better, he does not really believe that it is the medication that made him better, so he stops taking the medication and soon reverts back to the dark world of hallucinations, delusions, hearing voices, paranoia, and the many other comingled psychotic symptoms that constitute schizophrenia. Even when they are arrested for offences or crimes that they don't even realize they committed, they don't attribute it to their mental illness, but rather to their being victims of an unjust and unfair system that is targeting them for persecution."

Rebecca was impressed with the detailed knowledge that Ajay appeared to possess regarding this type of mental illness, and she was happy that she had learned something she was not aware of before. She had seen so many homeless people on the streets who often appeared to be talking to themselves. She made a mental note to think of them as *hearing voices* rather than *talking to themselves*. She never knew much about schizophrenia or the Catch-22 that Ajay just described so clearly.

"Then why doesn't the system take them off the streets, institutionalize them, and compel them to take the medications, so that they can stay out of trouble"?

"Excellent question, Becky.

Institutionalizing the mentally ill was common practice until the 60's. In the 60's and 70's our country decided to follow the path of deinstitutionalizing them. It made it close to impossible to commit anyone against their will. Deinstitutionalization successfully gave more rights to some of the mentally challenged, especially those with Downs syndrome and other mental disorders where the ill person had a reasonable chance of being integrated into society with a moderate level of care. Schizophrenics, unfortunately, did not fall into this category. The government decided to spend money on community mental health centers instead of asylums. The mid-70's movie, *One Flew over the Cuckoo's Nest,* symbolized the negative aspects of mental institutions and, in general, the public did not complain when institutionalization was done away with. There was no one to lobby for the schizophrenics who would have benefited more from the continuation of forced institutionalizing which could give them the long-term care they needed.

Thus, the ugly negative was that many of those released from institutions then, or never committed to institutions since, are on the streets today, and they are severely mentally ill. They are not good candidates for community centers due to the nature of their illnesses. For illnesses like schizophrenia, long-term in-patient care is sorely needed. This type of illness does not lend itself well to voluntary treatment by the patient himself, for the reasons I mentioned before. No voluntary self-treatment is possible if the recognition of one's illness is an issue. Another problem is that the mentally ill adult cannot adequately address even his normal physical ailments. He cannot check himself in for treatment of blood pressure, diabetes, heart or kidney or liver ailments like normal people. He is afraid to visit doctors, unaware of the seriousness of his condition, and therefore extremely prone to early and serious deterioration of his health and longevity. In other countries, you don't see so many people with different types of mental illness on the streets. The state institutionalizes and takes care of them, both mental and physical conditions. Leaving an adult schizophrenic to take care of himself is like leaving a one-year-old baby to take care of himself. Both are completely incapable of doing so. Yet nobody seems to care. The one-year-old gets taken care of, but the mentally ill remain marginalized. Our world is governed by and focuses on those who are lucky enough to be mentally normal."

Rebecca listened with rapt attention. Indeed, she had been to Europe several times and also to several Asian countries, and did not ever see so many mentally ill people on the streets. Poor people-yes, homeless-yes, but not mentally ill. Now she understood why. They were institutionalized. Rebecca's mother was a long time Alzheimer patient and she knew a fair amount about Alzheimer's and dementia but nothing about schizophrenia or the mental health care system surrounding this type of illness. She wondered how Ajay knew so much detail. She determined to ask him later. Before that, she had one more question.

"If their condition deteriorates when they are on the streets, then, surely, they can be taken to psychiatric hospitals, can they not? Then they can get the long-term inpatient care you were talking about."

"Aha, this brings us to the second Catch-22. It is true that the condition of these mentally ill people on the streets, especially those with severe schizophrenia, often deteriorates to the extent where their actions compel people around them to call the police or hospitals. The police, in most major cities, are usually trained to recognize mental illness, and will typically take them to Emergency Psychiatric care at a local hospital if it is just a question of aberrant behavior. Here they will be kept on hold for a few days, given medication, usually forcibly, and, here is the catch - *when they are judged to be back to almost normal, they must be released*. There is no way that they can get the really long-term care which they so desperately need. There is no legal way to hold them once they are somewhat back to normal. Before release, sometimes they are made to agree to take the prescribed medications, but there is no law or system that can force them to, as adults. It is totally voluntary. As it almost always happens, their mental illness soon relapses, they are back on the streets and the cycle begins again.

In fact, Becky, there is a worse-case scenario. Often, they break the law unknowingly. In their delusional, schizophrenic state they don't really know or understand what they are doing. In these cases, when the police are called, they are taken, not to the psychiatric hospital, but often to jail first. Then, after a few days, they are either released or made to appear in court where a public defender acts as their only advocate. In jail, sometimes they are given the medication they need, because some jails have sections dedicated to the mentally ill inmates, but often they don't get the treatment they need at the time they need it most. This is really a failure of the system, in that, even though the police recognize that the person is mentally ill, they have to legally give priority to the fact that a law was broken and leave it up to the court system to consider mental illness as a mitigating factor. Getting treatment for the mental illness itself seems not to be a priority for the police. For other types of illness, the health factor would come first. If a criminal, caught in the act, were to have a heart attack, or even suspect one to be coming on, he or she would be taken to a hospital first, not to jail. One of the reasons for this reversal of priority may be that the system does not know or recognize the fact that very often the extreme manifestation of mental illness, that caused the illegal action, is simply due to lack of medication.

There are probably as many mentally ill people in our jail system today as in psychiatric hospitals.

Of course, the greatest number of them are on the streets. They cannot get jobs, or housing. Their families and friends have rejected them, and the street is the only life they know. They live in a different world, in an alternate reality, and they become the marginalized among us. It seems terribly unfair and wrong that our society is far from ideal in treating physical and mental illness on an equal footing.

Let me tell you one more shocking fact - there is no database at any level, country, state, county or city, which can be accessed by a mental health professional, to obtain the medical data on a mentally sick person, collected over time for different hospitalizations and treatments at different places. This, if available, could be really useful in recognizing past treatment that was effective and not having to experiment with different medications from scratch every time. Such a database is not so critical for other types of illness, because the patient can provide the relevant information to the care provider that will enable his prior record to be accessed. The mentally ill are incapable of providing this vital feedback on their own past medical history. The trial-and-error approach is the only one available for the psychiatric hospitals and, almost always, it results in a much longer time to recovery and much more pain to the ill person and his family and relatives."

Ajay stopped, had a sip of the water in front of him, and looked at Rebecca as if waiting for her acknowledgment and understanding.

Rebecca was fascinated by Ajay's knowledge of schizophrenics and their care, or lack thereof. Everyone knew about the homeless problem in cities like San Francisco, from reading about it or actually experiencing their presence on the streets, but this was the first time that she saw clearly the connection between mental illness and homelessness, and began to grasp the basic reasons why it was such a difficult problem to tackle. Severe mental illness and homelessness were inextricably linked, she realized. Even if the ill person came from a well to do family who were initially willing to take care of him or her, the fact that the ill person does not recognize his own illness would make it difficult, if not impossible, to stay within the confines of the family and he would be out on the streets, unaware of his illness and unaware of his connections to family or friends.

There was an intensity and passion in Ajay's explanations that indicated in-depth personal experience. There was a tinge of pain and frustration when he talked about the failure of the system to protect schizophrenics which indicated that Ajay or someone close to him was fighting a battle, a battle he knew the boundaries of, but had not yet won. When Ajay stopped talking, Rebecca noticed a relaxed expression on his face and eyes, the look of a man who had achieved a deeper level of understanding and come to terms with whatever his personal situation was. Rebecca suspected that there was no way he could be so passionately knowledgeable without being personally involved in some way. She had to find out more about him, but she needed to be careful in how she asked the question that was on her mind for quite some time. She looked at him and asked in a low voice,

"Ajay, how come you know so much about schizophrenia and the health-care system connected with mental illness? Hope you don't mind my asking!".

Ajay thought for a while before answering. He was expecting the question, as it was a reasonable one. Rebecca was a total stranger which made it relatively easy to tell her his deeply personal story. People tend to keep personal secrets from close friends and relatives, but strangers could be trusted more. Such is the paradox of sharing secrets.

"Becky, my son was diagnosed with schizophrenia over a decade ago!"

Rebecca was stunned and slightly embarrassed.

"Oh, I am so sorry", she blurted out.

"Oh no, no need to be sorry, I have been dealing with this for the past dozen or so years and the situation is always evolving, always challenging, always a mixture of hope and frustration, ups and downs. I may appear to know a fair amount, but actually I am constantly learning, and there is a lot more to learn".

Rebecca kept quiet. She looked at the time on her smartphone. It was too late for doing anything else and still too early for dinner. It was not too chilly although the shadows had begun to lengthen and a light breeze was blowing from the direction of the Golden Gate Bridge. The office goers, tourists and hawkers were all still there. The essence of Union Square was unchanged although the individual people were changing constantly. She clearly remembered the gestures and shuffling gait of the homeless man they had both seen and who had triggered this conversation with Ajay. It seemed to her that she had seen the homeless man a thousand times over the years. The same or a similar story repeated endless times. Who knew where the man was now, and what voices he was hearing in his head?

"I have some more time. I would like to chat a bit more", said Rebecca, Then, without waiting for Ajay, she went on,

"I have lived through tough times the last two years. My mother has dementia, and I am her caregiver. I feel that your situation is much more challenging, and if I could, I would like to know more about your son. If you don't want to talk any more about him, that is perfectly OK too."

Ajay smiled and said: "I don't mind talking a bit more. A sympathetic ear is not easy to find, and not many people know my story. I am very sensitive to the fact that often people show some level of interest in other people's situations but without the deeper empathy that can really make a difference. I sense that you do have that empathy, Becky, so I will continue".

"It started over twelve years ago, when my son was twenty-five. I was on a business trip to Thailand, and had just arrived at Bangkok when I saw a message from our local hospital back home. The caller ID said Santa Clara Valley Medical Center. *Please call this number. Your son, Raj, wants to talk with you*, the message said, giving the number and an extension. My first reaction was that Raj had been involved in an accident, and I was glad that he was at least in a condition where he could talk with me. After I reached the hotel, I called the hospital. It was the Emergency Psychiatric section that I reached. *Why psychiatric?* I wondered. *Maybe he had trauma as a result of the accident*, I tried to guess. I asked for Raj by name. When he came on the line and said hello, I recognized his voice. It sounded tense.

Hi Raj, this is Dad, I said, hoping to start a conversation that would comfort and reassure him that I was there for him. His response hit me square in the guts.

My name is John, who are you? I don't recognize you,

I am your dad. You are Raj, not John, I replied.

I am John, what is your name? he asked.

I gave him my full name and said,

Raj, you are my son.

Really? he said with incredulousness in his tone,

Then why don't I have you in my head?

His speech was a little slurred and his voice sounded a bit different, as though he was sedated. I had to think quickly on my feet. My brain was in a whirl. What the hell had happened to Raj? I decided to try a different tack,

What happened? Why are you there?

I don't know why I am here either. I was talking with someone on the street in front of my apartment, and they called the police on me. They brought me here three days ago.

Three days? I said in surprise. Why didn't you call me earlier?

I just told you I don't even know who you are. You are telling me you are my dad, but I don't know anyone with that name. The hospital people found your number in my wallet and asked me to call you. By the way, you should call me John. Bye now.

With that he hung up and I sat on my hotel bed with my head in my hands, thinking,

What a disaster, how could this be happening? What has happened to his brain? Could it be drugs? I knew that he had experimented with drugs in high school and college. Will he ever become normal again? Will we ever get him back? What should I do now? Many questions, no answers, nowhere to seek advice, no one to talk to. It was close to midnight in Bangkok. I had a full day of work scheduled for the next day, I was tired, and I was so far from California.

I began to think about recent interactions I had with Raj and time we had spent together over the past few weeks. Some strange incidents now suddenly became relevant. One day, after we had lunch together at a restaurant, and on the way to dropping him off at his apartment, Raj told me that one of the waiters in the restaurant was very likely a foreign spy, and that several people in the restaurant where we just ate were plotting against us. I was a bit surprised.

"How do you know?", I asked him. He said that he had seen the same guy in a 7-11 store a few days ago and he was acting very suspiciously.

"It is so obvious! Didn't you notice anything, Dad?"

I firmly said "No, I didn't notice anything at all, and I don't think anyone was plotting anything against us."

"Just be careful!" he advised me.

I didn't quite know how to handle these weird comments and attributed them to some recent instance of substance abuse. *He will get over it soon*, I remember telling myself. Ajay paused and looked at Rebecca, "Am I going into too much detail? Let me know if I am".

"Of course not, please go on".

Rebecca could feel his sense of shock at his son not recognizing him on the phone. She remembered the times when her mother barely recognized her. This was the first time that she was listening to such a first-hand experience of mental illness.

"What did you do next?" she could not help asking.

Ajay continued,

"Although I was very tired with my head hurting from lack of sleep, I decided to call the Hospital again after a while, and this time ask the Hospital personnel details about his case. I was directed to a case worker who was assigned to Raj. These case workers, I found out later, provide personal attention, care and guidance to mentally ill patients. They are part of the care system in psychiatric wards, sort of in between the patient and the psychiatrist, similar to the role of nurses in regular hospitals. He told me that Raj approached a lady who was in a car near his apartment. The lady recognized that he was in need of psychiatric help, and called the police. The police, trained to spot the mentally ill, took him to EPS at Santa Clara Valley Medical Center."

"What does EPS stand for?

"EPS stands for Emergency Psychiatric Services. They gave him some medications and he is much calmer, compared to his condition when he was brought in three days ago. The case worker was nice enough to offer to give me updates if I called him during his shift, which I agreed to do. I called a friend who knew Raj, and requested him to visit Raj and see what his condition was and report back to me the next day. He reported back that Raj seemed to recognize him but stayed far away and there was no communication. I had to take a sleeping pill that night to help me fall asleep and be reasonably alert for a full day's work the next day.

My work in Ayutthaya, near Bangkok, kept me busy the following day and I surprised myself that I was able to focus on work. No one around me had any clue about the traumatic situation I was in. Interactions with colleagues, especially on business trips, are continuous and intense. You spend over ten hours a day with the same people and you think you know everything about them. Yet, they may have deeply hidden secrets and problems in their personal lives which you cannot even begin to imagine, like mine. I called the Hospital again the next day and got Raj on the line. This time his voice sounded more normal. His speech was a little less indistinct. I felt that he half-recognized me, although he never clearly said so. He again asked me my full name and how I spelled it. When I asked him about what he said the last time we talked, he said in a conspiratorial way that he knew who I was all the time, but to prevent my being hurt by outside forces who were listening in on our conversation, had pretended that I wasn't his dad, and also did not admit to his real name. He asked me to be careful and avoid the fate that befell him. He was watching TV, he said, when

Zap! something happened and they had taken over my brain, and the next thing I knew I was here.

I did not press him. He was a bit more articulate, although still paranoid. I told him I would be back home in a few days, and would go to visit him if he was not discharged by then. I called the case worker every day to get an update. The case worker said that the regular medication was helping to improve his condition a little bit every day. He was slowly coming back into the real world from the delusionary world he was in. That explained why he made up a reason for not recognizing me and calling himself by another name. He said Raj's diagnosis was 'psychosis non-specific' which stood for a wide range of mental illnesses in which psychosis occurred. I googled it. It was a broad categorization and allowed them to treat him with some modern antipsychotic medications.

After a few days, I returned home. When I called the case worker, he told me that the medications had apparently brought him back close to normal, but they wanted to keep him on hold for a few days longer. However, he wanted to get out earlier. They have a court system whereby he presents his case for being allowed to go, and the hospital doctors present their arguments for keeping the hold on him, and a 'judge' decides whether he can get out or not. If the decision is negative, he has to wait for a couple of more days to appeal again."

"Why don't the doctors just make their decision and do whatever they think is best for him?" asked Rebecca.

Ajay took some time before replying.

"I have never really asked them that, but I suppose it is because they want to be sure that the patient's rights are exercised, especially because, unlike other illnesses, mental illness is harder to quantify. The ill person cannot be trusted to be objective enough. Whether a person is better or not becomes a subjective judgment by others around him, hence the court system. I suppose they want to avoid the legal issues that may arise if the person says he was held against his will, even though he was fine."

"Do you have any other children?", Rebecca suddenly asked.

"Yes, a daughter. We are very close. She has her own family, with kids, and lives in the East coast. Although she knows everything now, at that time I decided to tell no one about Raj's mental condition. I needed to deal with it myself first."

Ajay continued after a brief pause,

"The case worker invited me to be at the hospital at the time of his release. There were four people in the room. Raj, his attending psychiatrist, the case worker, and another lady who was either a nurse or a doctor. Raj looked quite normal, and I was relieved. The psychiatrist told me that he was brought in with severe psychosis. However, over the past few days his condition had improved with the medications he was given. Raj had apparently argued quite coherently and articulately about why he should be let go. I was not surprised. He was an ace debater in high school and part of winning debate teams. He was being released on the condition that he would see an outside psychiatrist regularly and follow his advice. She looked at Raj to see if he understood and agreed. Raj nodded. She emphasized the importance of the medications, gave him a few tablets which would last about a week, and a prescription to start him off.

On the way to his apartment, I told Raj how relieved I was that we had gotten him back. He didn't say anything. I dropped him off and went home and fell asleep quite early, still jet-lagged from the trip.

Over the next few months Raj began seeing a psychiatrist. I offered to go along with him, and for the first couple of sessions he agreed with my accompanying him. The psychiatrist diagnosed him with schizophrenia as the cause of his psychosis, and prescribed similar medications as the hospital had given him, and asked Raj to take them daily. Also, he set up regular monthly meetings with him to be able to monitor his condition. I read everything I could lay my hands on about psychosis, schizophrenia, and other related illnesses and soon felt confident and competent enough to talk to the psychiatrist about the disease and its symptoms and the medications that controlled it, and how the medications worked. I learned that typically the first symptoms appear in the late teens and I now remembered that Raj did indeed show many of the early signs, which, of course, I did not recognize at that time. I also learned that the diagnosis and treatment of mental illness is not as precise and scientific as other illnesses. How the human brain works is one of the last frontiers in medical science. I also learned about different combinations of medications and the effectiveness as well as the side effects of different doses. I could talk knowledgeably about modern atypical antipsychotics working on serotonin neurotransmission instead of dopamine. The incomplete and imprecise level of scientific understanding of the root cause of schizophrenia was the equalizer that made me almost as competent as the best psychiatrists.

For three months or so, things were pretty normal. The strange episode was behind us and I began to hope that things would soon return to normal. Raj and I went to dinner roughly once a week. He was never very communicative, and seldom smiled, but at least he was not showing any strong signs of paranoia or delusions. Sometimes he would remind me about how accomplished he was at high school in debate or some other area. I readily agreed with him, realizing that perhaps he was trying to get some consolation for himself that he was once normal and accomplished. We started talking about jobs he might apply for or other activities he may pursue. Then suddenly everything fell apart".

"What happened?" Rebecca asked in a low voice.

"First, he stopped seeing the psychiatrist, and stopped taking his medication. After a little over a week of no contact, I woke up one morning and saw that there were about thirty text messages from him. The messages were garbled, incoherent, full of vitriolic obscenities that I cannot even begin to tell you. It was clear that Raj was in the grip of psychosis. I never knew or could have ever imagined the type of incoherent obscenities that I read that morning. I immediately texted him back, asking if he had taken the medications regularly. In reply there was another stream of obscenities and threats. I stayed calm and repeatedly told him to take the medications, but I don't think my pleas registered. Some more garbled, incoherent texts and then he stopped texting. I made up my mind to try to contact him again around dinner time, hoping that he would have taken his medications, and went about my daily routine, trying to forget the words of his texts. In a way this was not very hard, because the words were so extreme that it was easier to ignore, than if they were more sensible. There was no response to my texts that evening. I did not initiate any more contact with him, nor did I hear from him for a couple of days. Then I tried texting him again - no response. Tried calling - his phone seemed dead because the call went straight to voicemail. I began to worry. I went to his apartment, he wasn't there. A third and a fourth day went by, and I was getting ready to call the police and hospitals in the area when I got a call from a hospital in Monterey County, near Salinas. It was almost a two-hour drive from his home. He was in their Emergency Psychiatric ward, and wanted to talk to me"

"How did he get to Salinas? Why Salinas?"
"I could never find out all the details, but let me tell you in summary what I found out by talking to Raj, the hospital authorities and the local police. It seems that in the middle of the night, hearing voices in his head, he suddenly felt paranoid and wanted to *flee to somewhere safe*. He started driving on the highway without thinking about exactly where he was headed. He was definitely driving at unsafe speeds to escape from whatever demons he envisaged were after him. When he saw a small local airport, he decided to try to fly to Las Vegas, not even realizing that the airport was closed at that hour, and the airplanes he could see inside were small private planes, not commercial jetliners. He tried to enter the airport past security and was stopped. The Highway Patrol was called and, after listening to his incoherent and delusional words, that he was an ex-Army veteran, and was going to Las Vegas because he had an appointment with a movie star, they took him to the psychiatric ward of the hospital nearby and impounded his car. He had his German shepherd with him in the car. He had gotten the dog a few months earlier without my knowledge and she was his constant companion. The police took her to an animal shelter. Although he got the dog back when he was released from hospital, she was finally taken away from him a year later because the police were convinced that he could not properly take care of her.

I went to visit him the next day. The psychiatrist in charge asked me what his history was, including his medication history. He said he would like to change the medications Raj was being given and wanted my suggestion as to which medication and what dosage may be best for him based on my observations regarding their effectiveness. *This totally surprised me.* Why wouldn't they have a database where his psychiatric treatment record would be accessible? A regular medical doctor would *never* ask a non-medical person like me something like that! I began to sense some of the inherent problems in providing adequate care for the mentally ill. As the years would go by, my understanding as well as frustrations would be sharpened a lot more. In any case, the psychiatrist told me that he would follow the prescription which had worked during the previous episode, and thanked me for the information.

It took Raj a week at the emergency unit to recover. They had started out with a heavier than usual dose of the prescribed antipsychotic and then phased it down as he improved. I visited him almost daily. There was a blank look in his eyes during the first few days, although he did recognize me. The blank look disappeared after a few days and he was more normal towards the end of his stay. Before I went to finally pick him up from the hospital, I drafted a list of items I wanted him to promise to adhere to and put it in writing, like taking daily medication, reducing smoking and alcohol intake, etc. Of course, I knew full well that it would be difficult, if not impossible, to enforce these promises, but at least he would be aware that he made them, and it was better than nothing. His previous psychiatrist had told me to ignore his smoking and drinking for the time being, since we were tackling much more serious problems first. I got his car back from impound, picked up the dog, and took him back home. The expenses incurred with the car and dog were high, but paled into insignificance when I thought about bringing Raj back. It was a long drive back, and I wanted to get into his mind, his mental state and what he was thinking when he was taken in. Raj answered each question in staccato fashion. He had not been able to sleep for several nights because of hearing persistent voices in his head. He supposed that insomnia was his basic problem. According to Raj, he couldn't sleep, and therefore he became crazy and heard voices. He smelled and even saw things that weren't there, and finally the fear of the voices and what they were saying became so intense that he had to get into his car and try to escape. That was over a week ago. He was much better now. I asked him if he still heard voices after the hospital treatment.

"They never go away. They remain subdued. They are always there. Dad, I am *never alone* even when you may think I am. They are always saying something to me. I just wish I could, even for one day, be like my old self, be just by myself. Just me in my head, no one else there".

I was deeply saddened by that comment and realized how different the reality of a schizophrenic was. He told me that someday he would really want to fly to meet his girlfriend who is a film actress, somewhere in Hollywood or Las Vegas. I kept quiet. He suddenly asked me if I was really his father. I calmly answered in the affirmative. Then he told me that our family should not patronize Holiday Inns because, when he wanted to check in, they refused to allow him to stay. Given his condition on the day he was taken to the hospital, I could easily understand why no hotel would allow him in. Again, I did not say anything, except that I had always felt welcome at Holiday Inns. In this and future communications with him, based on my discussions with psychiatrists and mental health care providers, I followed the path of non-confrontation combined with sticking to a logical and sane point of view, firmly contradicting or refuting delusional statements as much as possible, with as few words as possible, and keeping quiet if I perceived a strong and unreasonable reaction. I asked Raj if he was taking the prescribed medications regularly before this last episode. His answer came as a bit of a surprise.

I really don't have schizophrenia. Didn't you know that those medications are just placebos? Also, they affect my ability to have sex.

He was in denial even after just getting out of the hospital and did not realize the inherent contradiction in his statements. If the medications were indeed placebos, they would not have side effects. The hospital had brought his psychosis under control with the same medications that he was in denial of. I knew that sexual dysfunction was one of the known side effects of the antipsychotic medications, but he didn't have any relationships that I was aware of, so I was a bit surprised that he considered that to be an important factor. After a few minutes of silence, he admitted that the voices became much more subdued when he took the medications, but he felt like a zombie. *The intense crazy delusional feeling without medications was sometimes actually preferable*, he said. It was like a psychotic high. Through these conversations I had begun to realize the enormous complexity of the problem we were facing. We finally reached his apartment where I left him after getting him some essentials from a nearby store."

Rebecca was listening intently, and had not spoken a word. The incidents Ajay described happened many years ago. She was getting curious about what was going on with Raj now. Did he recover? Did he get worse? She decided to just let Ajay tell his son's story at his own pace. Suddenly Ajay said,

"Becky, we have spent a long time here. It is getting towards evening. Maybe we should call it a day and meet again some other day?"

Rebecca wanted to hear more, but it was indeed getting late. Her mother's caretaker would be looking for relief, so she had to get back.

"Yes, let's exchange contact information and meet again sometime soon. Your story is fascinating. I have so many thoughts, so many questions, but they have to wait till next time, I suppose".

Lights shone through many of the hotel and shop windows surrounding Union Square. Sometimes a shadow would pass across a window, people walking inside their rooms, probably shutting down for the day. Union Square itself was still full of people, walking this way and that, intersecting physical space but not interacting with each other, unaware that two people in their midst had just shared such in-depth personal experiences with mental illness and its complexities. As Ajay walked towards the subway station, he felt that the conversation with Becky had been quite useful. This was the first time he had gone into so much detail of Raj's case with anyone. By narrating his experiences and answering her questions, he actually had gained a better overall understanding of his son's situation, and his own reactions to it. He wished to tell her more, about the time Raj was arrested for being violent, about the time he was actually homeless for a few days on the streets of San Francisco, and about the time when he was violent towards Ajay, on a Thanksgiving night, and Ajay had to call the police to restrain Raj, and they took him away. There was also the time when he told Ajay how much he loved and respected him and that Ajay was the best Dad in the world. Such are the contradictions that become the new normal in the world of schizophrenia.

Little did Ajay know, as a cool San Francisco breeze sprung up that evening, that a new and deadly virus lurked, waiting to prey on mankind, and this virus would soon take over and control the affairs of man in a way no one had seen or foreseen, in this or the previous generation. The Covid-19 pandemic was still a couple of months away from even being a scare. There was no premonition of what was to strike mankind a few weeks later and upend lives everywhere. It is a great blessing that future catastrophes are never revealed to us ahead of time. Only those future events, like the weather, that are a simple and direct follow on or continuation of what is happening today can ever be predicted by us.

The O'Farrell subway station was just a few minutes' walk, and Ajay enjoyed the fast pace he set himself. The health monitor on his smartphone would give him credit for meeting his steps quota for the day, thought Ajay. Then his mind went back to Raj. He usually avoided thinking about Raj, only reacting to events and actions as necessary. This was not because of indifference, or apathy, or lack of empathy. It was the sheer instinct of self-survival combined with a broader view of what was in Raj's overall best interests. Raj needed him for as long as possible and, therefore, he had to be in good health and spirits, to be there for Raj. He could not afford to let himself down, for that would be letting Raj down. He had learned this from his father. His father had to look after his mother lifelong. One day, as a child, Ajay had asked him how come he almost never got sick. His father laughingly said,

"Son, because I cannot afford to get sick. Who will look after your mother?"

Although Ajay's father intended his comment to be in jest, Ajay, even at an early age, realized the deeper truth behind his dad's comment, that our way of thinking, our approach to problems can make the difference. Attitude counts.

Since the first episode twelve years ago, Ajay had hoped many times that Raj would be able to lead a close to normal life as long as he took medications and stayed in a controlled environment, but that was not to be. Raj was in police custody or hospitals about a dozen times over the years and each such incident had its own danger and drama and was fraught with the uncertainty of not knowing how it would end. The possibility of Raj's life ending in a violent way was always within the realm of possibility.

There were times in between episodes when their relationship was closer to normal. Raj would ask to spend time with Ajay doing something together, like playing miniature golf. They would go out to a public miniature golf course and Ajay felt happy and proud that he and Raj were behaving somewhat like father and son engaged in a sport or hobby together. Then the game would be over and after buying dinner for Raj and dropping him home, Ajay would be left to wonder what the next day would bring. Ajay had learned long ago to live the 'Raj' part of his life one day at a time. Anything else would be too unrealistic or wishful.

Raj was an excellent driver in his younger years, but the schizophrenia made him total three cars over a period of five years and finally his driver's license was taken away, not for any of these accidents but for a drunk driving charge for which he failed to show up in court. There was a warrant out for his arrest but he had deluded himself into thinking that he had talked to *higher authorities* and resolved his case. He always thought that he was framed for the infraction and should have gotten his license back. He was evicted from several apartments he lived in and Ajay often put him up in hotels while trying to find his next apartment. That was a challenge in itself, because Raj was not qualified to rent, so Ajay had to sign and vouch for him. Ajay ended up with huge expenses caused by Raj's destroying many of the rental properties during psychotic fits. Often, when Raj was in a psychotic state, he would post all sorts of crazy nonsense about his high school friends on Facebook, or other social media, accusing them of being foreign spies, or perpetrators of deviant acts. At first his friends were angry, because they thought Raj was just being bad. Then, when they realized that he had a severe mental illness, they would feel sorry for him. A few of them offered to help, but eventually everyone had their own lives to lead and they slowly withdrew from any contact with him. One of his friends stuck with him longer than others, but finally even he gave up when Raj aggressively accused him of interfering with his life. His friends would contact Ajay and discuss what to do. Ajay told them there was not much to be done, except hope that Raj would take the medications and remain somewhat stable. Slowly, he lost his friends one by one. His high school sweetheart had left him long ago, but he still missed her. He completely destroyed one of the several rented apartments he lived in, breaking the walls and scrawling threats and obscenities on every possible space in every wall. He destroyed his TV, his games and toys, but there was one thing he did not destroy. It was a painting his girlfriend had given him as a gift, which was carefully preserved. She was his one and only sweetheart. She had left him around the same time when he began to exhibit the first symptoms of psychosis, and because of that reason, he had never fully grasped why she left him. Ajay discovered the painting when having his apartment cleaned up after Raj was hospitalized and thereafter evicted. Ajay decided to keep it as a memory, but for whom? It was a reminder of a love lost, but the person who lost it probably did not want to remember and would feel excruciating pain at the memory. Nevertheless, Ajay felt that the memory was worth preserving, if only for its own sake, if only just because Ajay knew its history. It was interesting that even within the framework of distorted perceptions and psychotic brain functions, the memory of a lost love could be preserved.

The only person that Ajay could communicate with regarding Raj, was his daughter Rini, his first born, who was living in the East Coast. Ajay loved Rini deeply and sometimes felt guilty that after he lost Raj to mental illness, he often consoled himself by thinking that he was glad he still had his beloved Rini. When Raj had his first problems with psychosis, Rini was single and working at a consulting firm. Ajay at first had shielded Rini from Raj's illness, but finally told her all the details. Ajay still remembers the day when Rini asked him, "Dad, so I do not have a brother any more"? The poignancy and finality of that comment was heartrending, but Rini had the strength of mind to not let Raj's situation affect her life. She continued to have a successful career, got married to a great guy, had children and even kept up occasional contact with Raj. Raj made a heroic effort to remain stable with medication and was able to attend Rini's wedding. Unfortunately, a couple of years after that, during one of his episodes, he said some things to her that made her block his communications, but she kept herself open to a possible reconnect if Raj's mental condition improved and remained stable. Ajay remembered the days when Raj and Rini were toddlers and they would be playing and fighting and laughing and crying, like children everywhere, until Raj's illness took him away on a different path, where he was alone in one sense but *never alone* in another.

From a few cases to hundreds of millions, the coronavirus took its toll on everyone over the next year and a half. Ajay worked from home and reflected on how the pandemic had affected the world order. Much was written and said about jobs lost, effect on world economies and the slow workings of pharmaceutical research and drug development that was delaying both a vaccine and a cure. Finally, the vaccines came and life returned to a moderate level of normalcy, but not much was ever discussed about how the pandemic affected the mentally ill, those who were incapable of fully realizing its deadliness. Fortunately, Raj, even in his reduced capacity, took excessive precautions, although he seldom ventured out.

It was during the early days of the pandemic that the latest and most traumatic episode occurred. After being evicted from his last apartment, Raj had appeared to be relatively stable in his new abode for over one year, which was surprising because Ajay knew he had not been taking medications for a long time. Then the inevitable happened. He began to spiral out of stability and into the psychotic state which characterized his relapses. Ajay was sensitive to changes in the language and tone and content of the text messages which Raj sent to him when he was beginning to get worse. He implored Raj to start taking his medications and offered to take him to psychiatric hospital, but to no avail. By the time the psychosis affected his text messages, Raj was deep into the spiral, and on the verge of danger.

About two years earlier he was hit by a car while crossing a street near the hotel where he was staying at the time, which had rendered him disabled. His hip was broken, and although he received emergency care at the local hospital, he was unable to focus on follow up procedures and remained long term disabled, unable to walk without support. Raj bought books and researched online on how to become an orthopedic surgeon, so he could heal himself. Ajay brought him lunch and dinner every day, and drinks and other necessities as and when requested. These visits had become a part of Ajay's life and all his other activities were scheduled around these food and supplies drop offs to Raj.

Unknown to Ajay, Raj had purchased some BB guns which, he claimed, were to protect himself from imaginary enemies who were out to harm him. As his schizophrenia worsened and psychosis took over, he walked around his neighborhood with his BB gun. The gun looked real, and the neighbors called the police. The police called Ajay to alert him. This was the second time for such an incident. They told Ajay that they were headed to his apartment. It was Father's Day and Raj had sent Ajay a rambling text message earlier in the day offering to take Ajay out for lunch. Ajay had ignored the message because it was clear from the words and tone of the message that Raj was in no condition to get out of the apartment, let alone go to a restaurant to have lunch. The police Sergeant in charge of the unit told Ajay that this time it was serious because several neighbors had complained and the police could not take any chances. As long as the guns looked real, he could not be walking around with them. He could easily get shot and there would be little recourse because it is legal to shoot someone if the shooter feels his life is in danger. The police could shoot him too and there were incidents like this in recent months in several states where people were shot and killed. *BB guns that look like real guns should not really be available for sale*, Ajay thought, but that was a different topic. In this country even real guns were so easily available. The paradox is that real guns can only cause harm in the hands of those who intend to harm, but BB guns, mistaken for real guns, can much more easily cause harm to those who carry them, the innocent or the mentally ill.

When Ajay arrived at the apartment, a surreal scene met his eyes. All streets were blocked off. There were several policemen with their rifles trained on Raj's shuttered window and locked door, standing behind an armored car that looked like a tank, using it as a shield. Ajay's heart was beating fast and his throat felt dry. This was a scene that could be straight from a movie, except no one knew where this would end up, how it would go. Ajay was asked not to go near but wait for the Sergeant in charge and follow instructions. The Sergeant told Ajay that they wanted Raj to come out of the apartment, so they could search and seize all his BB guns since those guns posed a threat to himself and the community. Ajay thought it would actually be good if the police apprehended Raj and took him to the psychiatric hospital where he could get the medications he needed. He was told that they would take him to jail first and the jail had a psychiatric wing where he could be taken care of. Ajay was quite familiar with the psychiatric wing of jails, from a previous episode. About a year before this incident, for the first time in his life he had visited someone in jail, his own son!

The police had asked Raj to voluntarily come out of the apartment but he had refused. From the police's viewpoint, Raj was being difficult and posed a potential threat. From Raj's point of view, he was mortally afraid of the police, especially so when he was hearing voices, and the voices would often be telling him to be careful of people who were intending to harm him. He associated police with forcible restraint, painful handcuffing, and being taken to jail or hospital for days on end, for no good reason, according to his way of thinking. If you included delusions, the police may be appearing to Raj as monsters or demons, not as humans. To Ajay, on the other hand, the police were like a savior. When all else failed, and Raj was a threat to himself or to others, the police would find a way to get him treatment, before or after jail, something that Ajay could not do. The time in jail would often not last long because the judge would realize quickly that this was a case that needed medical attention rather than incarceration.

After several more unsuccessful attempts to get him to come out, the Sergeant asked Ajay if Raj and Ajay had any plans for Father's Day. Ajay mentioned the text that Raj had sent that morning. The sergeant then hatched a plan that went as follows. The police would get out of sight but remain nearby. Ajay would invite Raj out for a Father's Day lunch and if Raj agreed and got out of the apartment, they would apprehend him, search his place, take the BB guns and take him to jail and hospital in that order. Ajay argued that the hospital should come first, because his mental illness had to be taken care of. The Sergeant disagreed, and said the crime took precedence and then it was up to the judge as to the leniency of the sentence, based on his mental condition. Ajay asked if someone who was having a heart attack wouldn't be taken to hospital first. The Sergeant agreed he would, but mental illness was different. They both threaten life, Ajay thought, but let it go. Ajay agreed to play the role of decoy. The Sergeant gave Ajay detailed instructions:

"If he agrees to come out, first get his BB gun. Then ask him to sit in the back seat. Drive to the next street and park the car in the middle of the intersection. Get out of the car quickly, walk towards the next street and hand over the gun and car keys to the officer walking towards you, then continue walking towards the corner Starbucks."

Everything went as planned, until it didn't. Raj would not get out of the car and the police, for some reason, did not or could not enter the car to apprehend him. So, they kept asking him to come out with his hands in the air, and he kept yelling back that he can't hear them. Ajay was watching from a distance. Ajay told the police that when Raj is in a psychotic state, he hears voices that drown out any other sounds so it is possible that he could not understand the orders he was given. The Sergeant then asked Ajay to get a bit further away so he couldn't clearly see what was going on. Ajay knew that a K-9 unit had been called in and there was a dog circling the car. Ajay thought that the dog was there to sniff out illegal drugs. Ajay did not know that the dog had actually been brought in to bite Raj and drag him out of the car. The police had told Ajay everything except this part of the plan.

A crowd had gathered at the outskirts of the cordoned off zone and Ajay was part of that crowd. Suddenly there was a gasp from the crowd and screams of "Oh my God!" Ajay craned his neck and saw that the dog had Raj's upper left arm in his jaws and was dragging a yelling and crying Raj out of the car. As soon as Raj was laying on his side on the street, the dog was pulled off of him, he was handcuffed and made to sit on the sidewalk. Blood was pouring from his upper arm where the dog had bit him. Raj was sitting shaking his head, looking down at the street, and yelled just once, "Why did you do this to me?" Raj did not say one more word, did not cry and did not resist. Ajay felt a pain in his heart like he never felt before. He felt a strange mixture of guilt and hope. Guilt, that he had acted as decoy; and hope that Raj would get treated, and possibly try his best to avoid such a situation in the future.

About a year later, Ajay would find out that there was a big public outcry on racial bias in the use of police dogs and complaints from ER rooms in the Bay area that they were seeing an increasing number of people with flesh torn apart and sometimes with life threatening injuries from police dog bites. Recommendations would be made to hold off on the use of all canine units until the rules of engagement could be agreed on. All of the above were moot points for Ajay. He would never be able to erase from his mind that a dog was legally let loose on his son, a helpless schizophrenic and he could not do anything about it and the system did not seem to care.

The police ripped off Raj's shirt, bandaged the arm, and sent him off to Hospital Emergency where they said his bite would be taken care of. About two hours had elapsed from the time Ajay got to Raj's apartment to the time the EMS vehicle left. The police searched his apartment, found a few more BB guns, took them away, returned the car keys to Ajay and counseled him regarding how to prevent Raj from accessing BB guns in the future. Before Raj was taken away, Ajay made sure that the police knew that he was very ill and that the correct medication should be given as soon as possible. Ajay asked if he could contact the jail and inform them what medications Raj was on and should be taking. To his dismay, Ajay was told there was no way he could be allowed to communicate with any of the authorities in the jail or the psychiatric unit of the jail. This was in spite of the Sergeant acknowledging that there was no database where Raj's previously prescribed psychiatric medication list could be made available to the doctors who would be attending to him. All that Ajay could do was to scribble the name of the medication and the dosage on a piece of paper and request that the Sergeant give it to the appropriate person so that at least the doctors knew what he had been taking before. Ajay felt helpless, but it was a feeling he had at least a dozen times before. Raj was again evicted from the apartment for trashing the place on top of causing this disturbance with the police involved, and had no place to stay going forward. Still, Ajay felt a sense of relief. For the next few days Raj was out of his control, no longer his responsibility, no decisions to be made. The hospital would be taking care of him. Ajay could get on with his life's business until Raj was released and then the cycle would start again. Father's Day was behind him, it was a day the likes of which Ajay did not wish upon his worst enemy. It was almost exactly twelve years from Raj's first episode when Ajay was out of the country on business.

Raj spent a day at the Hospital ER where his wound was treated and then, after just a few hours in jail he was sent to a rehabilitation center in San Francisco which contacted Ajay to inform him that Raj was there. Apparently, Raj was eager to get out, but the attending psychiatrist felt that he was not ready yet. They called Ajay to update him on Raj's condition and status. When Ajay asked if Raj was being given the medications which Ajay knew worked for him, he was told that he was being given a different medication. Ajay knew that the medicine Raj was being given was not very effective at all, but his saying so had no effect. When Raj was finally released about ten days later, he was better than on Father's Day, but still far from stable. The bandage on his upper arm was a visible reminder of the police dog bite. While driving back from San Francisco, Raj was delusional about having a place to stay with 'friends' he had made at the hospital. Ajay dropped him off at a residential address as requested by Raj. The next day Raj asked to be picked up as there seemed to be a misunderstanding about either the address or whether he was welcome or not. The search for a new apartment began again.

Ajay eventually found another apartment for Raj and miraculously got Raj to agree to take medication which Ajay would give him every day when he brought him his lunch. This was a first. Previously Raj had very strongly objected to Ajay's interfering with his personal choice to take or not take medication. Raj had refused to even talk about his mental health issues. It was possible that the change in Raj's thinking was brought about by the trauma of the recent episode combined with his being evicted for the third time in five years. Whatever the reason, this was an opportunity for Ajay to give him, daily, the medication that worked. However, there was a new problem. How to get a continuing supply of the medication? Although Raj agreed to take the medication, he steadfastly refused to go to a doctor to get the medicine prescribed again. Ajay still had enough tablets left from previous prescriptions. He hoped that if Raj actually improved and got better, then he may change his mind about getting a new prescription. Alternatively, Ajay could try to get the medication from other sources without a formal prescription. The medication worked. Within a few days Raj was much better and more stable than when he left the hospital. It was frustrating for Ajay that the system had failed Raj and him so badly. Even when, based on previous experience, he had tried to help the doctors with the name of the right medication, they had given Raj something that did not work and did not even try to verify whether Ajay's input had any merit or not. As a result, Raj had suffered, and would have suffered a lot more if Ajay had not finally given him what clearly had worked well in the past. The antipsychotic medication Raj was taking had diabetes as a side effect and the hospital had recommended diabetes medication for him. Raj of course would not voluntarily take any medication at all and Ajay prioritized the antipsychotic medication, keeping the diabetes medication option in the back burner. Again, it was a sad reflection of society's inability to address the overall health of mentally ill people that such decisions were left to friends and family instead of medical professionals. There were, of course, days when Raj was psychotic and delusional. He would tell Ajay about mansions and cars he had owned. He would describe how his cars were stolen from him by evil people. Sometimes Ajay was one of those evil people, and sometimes his sister. He would ask Ajay to find the stolen cars and bring them back to him. Overall, however, the medications kept things under control, as long as Ajay was able to sense when to modify the dosage based on Raj's condition.

One day, after a long hiatus, Ajay received a "Hi" text from Rebecca. Over several text exchanges he learned that her mother had passed away during the pandemic. Although the cause of death was complications related to Covid, the real cause was her Alzheimer's. Shortly after her funeral, one of Rebecca's distant relatives had offered her a job in his company in Australia. Rebecca had decided to take him up on the offer, and had decided to move to Australia, planning to leave the following month. She figured that a change of scene would help her at this point in her life. She was very keen to hear about Raj and they agreed to meet at their old Union Square meeting place.

The deli had long since ceased operations because of the pandemic. Ajay waited for Rebecca in front of its shuttered doors, aware that this was probably going to be their final meeting. Talking to her about Raj had helped him. Talking about a complex life situation helps to put things in perspective, to understand oneself better, and to get encouragement to continue or change course if necessary. There was a low-profile wall bordering the square and it was the perfect height for sitting on. They sat on this wall and talked.

They talked about Raj, about Rebecca's mother, about her new job in Australia, and about Ajay's life. Rebecca said that although she was terribly distraught at her mother's loss, she was able to feel better thinking that, from her mother's perspective, it was probably best that she was out of her misery and pain. That resonated with Ajay. He had often tried to put himself in Raj's shoes when Raj was in a pathetic condition, raving, unable to control himself, unaware of pleasure or pain, semi-homelessly roaming the streets and talking to the voices in his head. Ajay often felt unbearable pain thinking about Raj's suffering. Then again, sometimes from Raj's perspective, from the things he said and the way he said it, he was perhaps not so unhappy. He was in a crazed delusional world, but thought he was normal and people around him were crazy and mistreating him or shunning him for no reason. No one would ever know Raj's thoughts exactly, but thinking thus lessened Ajay's pain. Ajay told Rebecca that although he was mentally tough and never let Raj's situation weigh him down much, once in a while he would let his guard down, and he would miss having a son who would hug him and call him *Dad* lovingly. He would miss having a normal son. A normal, friendly and loving Raj with a calm, relaxed, handsome face often featured in Ajay's dreams, but every time he would wake up to a different and much harsher reality.

Ajay and Rebecca talked for a long time. Then they fell silent and watched the people on Union Square for a few minutes. People-watching had led to their first meeting and first communication. Rebecca finally said,

"Ajay I have to go. Expecting a call from Australia. Before I leave, however, I want to tell you that I have never met anyone who can be so involved and yet so detached, so emotionless on the surface and yet so deeply passionate and emotional inside, so confident in the middle of a difficult situation, so forgiving and yet so practical. Raj is really lucky to have you as a father. Wish you both the best of everything".

Ajay responded, "Thank you, Becky. Actually, in a strange way, I also consider myself lucky. I am lucky I can help someone who really needs me, even if that someone is my son."

With that they said *good bye* and Ajay turned away and started walking towards the nearby parking garage. A light drizzle had begun on a cold December night. The street lights glistened on the concrete and metal surfaces and the few pedestrians walked faster than they normally would, towards the warmth of their homes. Ajay reached into his pocket, took out the little plastic bottle with Raj's medications and looked at it. Just a bottle with a few white pills. So ordinary, yet so powerful, in that they determined the boundary between sanity and craziness, between logic and delirium, between life and death. A stray dog ran by. The thought briefly flashed across his mind that that particular dog would not be able to bite Raj. He wondered what Raj was doing at that moment. Perhaps he was watching the DVD movie Ajay had bought him a few days earlier. Or perhaps he was resting. Hopefully the voices in his head were subdued for the time being. His current semi-stable period had lasted well over a year already. Ajay felt a languorous sense of happiness, knowing he could sleep peacefully that night. Tomorrow would be another day. All that anyone could predict is that it would be sunny, with just a ten percent chance of precipitation, and Ajay would make sure that Raj got his medication.

CLICK FOR ROMANCE

Success can often be defined as finding what you are not looking for

Tim hadn't heard from Ben, his flight companion, for almost a year. The long flight to Shanghai a year ago, and the conversation with Ben were still fresh in his memory. Had Ben been able to marry Riya in spite of her mother's objections? Was Ben's an online dating success story, or a disaster for the record books? He needed to contact Ben and find out, as soon as possible.

It was a year ago that Tim had met Ben, shortly after the United Airlines Boeing 787 had taken off from Chicago's O'Hare airport, bound for Shanghai. No stranger to Asia, Tim followed a routine on these long flights that helped avoid boredom. Knowing the time zone changes, he would coordinate his flight departure time and sleep schedule before the flight, such that flying to Asia, he would not sleep on the flight, arrive in the late afternoon, and go to sleep early in a comfortable hotel bed. Going to Asia, jet lag wasn't a big issue and, in any case, didn't last long. Returning home was much tougher. He worked for a major American pharmaceutical company and their China Headquarters was having problems competing with Chinese companies that priced their medicines much lower and bribed doctors to selectively promote Chinese equivalent products. It was a well-known tactic that all pharmaceutical companies had to contend with. Tim's mission on this trip was to share some strategies with the Chinese Sales teams that would help their competitiveness. Shanghai, a city of over 25 million people was under a strict Covid related lockdown until recently, but was now opening up to travelers with the lockdown lifted. Starting in Shanghai, he would go on to Beijing and Guangzhou to meet different groups with similar missions.

Tim tried to fly Business class whenever possible. That day, the seat next to Tim's was unoccupied when the plane took off, so he was looking forward to having more space around him. In a world dominated by the virus, it was better to have this space. Tim's enjoyment of the space didn't last long. As soon as the plane reached cruising altitude and the seat belt sign had been turned off, the stewardess appeared with a man, apparently from Economy class, and sat him down next to Tim.

"Hi, I am Ben, upgraded", said the man, extending a closed fist which Tim bumped with his and responded,

"I am Tim, not upgraded".

Ben laughed, and said,

"I like that. My type of guy!"

Ben was in his mid-40s, hair greying at the edges, with a boyish face and smile wrinkles around his eyes which probably came from the ready smile he seemed to have whenever he talked. Tim took an instant liking to Ben, and considered that if the seat next to him had to be occupied, he would rather have a friendly guy than an unfriendly one, on a long fifteen-hour flight.

After that brief introduction, they both retreated to their own worlds for a while, until the stewardess brought their drinks. Then Ben asked Tim whether he was going to Shanghai for business or pleasure. "For work, and you?"

"I am going to meet a girl who I think I will date, and possibly have a long-term relationship with", replied Ben. Both Ben and Tim knew that such a reply would definitely go begging for further elucidation, so, as if on cue, Tim said,

"What, Wow, Awesome! Tell me more!"

"Tim, are you at all familiar with the online dating scene?"

"No not at all. I have been married twice, and am single now. I have dated several women, but never went online to find my date".

Ben went on, "I was married twice also, and then a friend of mine introduced me to possibilities online about three years ago, and I have found it quite interesting. It has led me to quite a few adventures, including this trip. I can go on forever if you let me".

"Not sure about forever, but I am a good listener, go ahead".

"OK, but first let me tell you a bit about myself."

Ben worked for an Architecture firm in Chicago. Born in upstate New York, of immigrant Jewish parents, Ben was brought up in a conservative and strict household that stressed frugality and excellence in education. He was not encouraged to date until he entered college, which was far later than any of his friends. His mother regarded dating strictly as a prelude to marrying the girl he would date. From his middle school years, he had learned to credit his classmates who were taller, smarter, better looking or simply more aggressive than himself with the natural ability to attract girls. He would listen to the stories of their exploits not so much with envy, but with a feeling that they belonged to a different world, not the world his parents had brought him up in. In college he tried to date a few women who had shown interest in him, unsuccessfully. His self-esteem was low. Ben was not only shy in approaching girls himself, but even when a girl would make the first move, he was seldom able to recognize it, and even if he did, almost never be able to follow through and make any progress. It was a triple whammy. Finally, as often happens with men like him, his family helped him find a suitable woman for marriage. She was from a good family, with a similar educational and social background and, perhaps not coincidentally, also did not have much experience or success in dating. They went out to a few dinners and had a few long conversations. Several months passed by, with nothing more happening except more dinners and more conversations. Their parents watched with consternation and kept prodding for action. Then one day Ben brought up the topic of marriage.

"Do you think we should tell them we plan to get married?" Ben asked in a way that a negative response wouldn't be too embarrassing.

"Why not?" his future wife said.

He was unhappy with the marriage virtually from day one. He often wished they had spent more time together, possibly lived together before tying the knot. Oftentimes he would blame his parents for pressuring him. Then, after two years, after a big fight, he suddenly decided that he had enough. One weekend, on a cold, snowy night, he packed two suitcases, booked a hotel in Indianapolis, and went to his car parked in the driveway, planning to brave the inclement weather and drive to a better future.

As fate would have it, his in-laws who lived about an hour away from them, unexpectedly showed up just as he was about to leave.

"Hey Ben, great seeing you. Where are you going on a night like this?" his father-in-law asked.

"That unexpected visit cost me three more years of my life!" he told Tim, with a laugh.

Tim had encountered similar situations, when a chance event altered the course of his life.

He shook his head and said,

"Well put!".

"My second marriage was completely my decision, and mine alone", Ben went on.

"My parents were hands-off and, understandably, did not want to risk getting blamed a second time. She was a colleague at work and we dated for a year. I was more experienced this time around and we both felt that we knew each other well enough for her to move in with me at my Lake Shore Drive two-bedroom apartment overlooking Lake Michigan. After a year of living fairly happily together, we decided we both wanted children and to get married."

"Sounds pretty ideal, so far", said Tim, anticipating a turn in events, since he already knew the end of this story.

"Yes, it was pretty ideal until we discovered that she could not have a successful pregnancy due to some rare medical complications. We went to several specialists over the course of three frustrating years, but to no avail. I accepted the situation better than my wife. Neither she nor I wanted to adopt. Finally, she told me on our fourth New-Year's eve together, that she wanted me to have a chance of having a child of my own and maybe we should live separately for a while, and see how that went. I agreed.

About seven months after that she told me that she had started dating an older man who had a grown son and did not want any more children. We divorced soon after that".

Shortly after the divorce, Ben reconnected with a high school friend who was also working in Chicago. This friend had been into online dating for several years and explained how it worked. He shared some opinions on various websites and explained the pros and cons to Ben. Ben was hesitant at first but decided to give it a try, having *nothing to lose*, as his friend said.

"It made a lot of sense. Suddenly hitherto invisible women from all over the world became visible. It was as if hidden treasures were revealed and choices opened up that never existed before. I could instantly meet women who I could never know or meet in several lifetimes. I could see them on video, chat with them, and then if things clicked, I could meet them in person and go from there. There are three stages to any successful relationship. The introduction, the spending time together and the longer-term life together. As far as the introduction, it was clear that online dating has a huge advantage in terms of a wider range of options. One could choose from a much larger field of potentially attractive partners, than otherwise possible. Spending time together was a challenge if the couple was separated geographically, but it was a challenge that could be dealt with. The longer-term prospect was the same as in any relationship, it depended on the ability of the individuals to handle the complexity of the forces tending to break the relationship apart."

Ben soon realized that there were many different types and genres of the online dating scene and he could immerse himself into any one or try multiple avenues. He tried and quickly eliminated the instant like-dislike type sites which were primarily intended for hook-ups or short-term relationships. Then there were sites which provided matchmaking services. They would ask you for all types of personal information and promise to provide you with a few good matches every day and you could study the women's profiles and take it from there. Alternatively, they could arrange group lunches, dinners or coffee dates. Then there were the international dating sites. Broken down by country and ethnicity these offered endless possibilities for the man seeking a relationship with a non-American woman. There were women from all European, African, Asian and South American countries, all looking for love at the click of a mouse any time during day or night.

"Do they speak English?" Tim asked.

"There are many funny stories regarding language. It was only after chatting with a Chinese woman for almost a week that I realized she could not understand or write even one word of English. She was using a translator software. One day I said that I would like to *call her bluff on her offer* to visit her hometown in China. Surprisingly this upset her. It took me a while to find out that the translator had told her that I thought she was a liar and she would have to pay for my trip to visit her. It was as if the translator had an impish mind of its own! Another translator gaffe was when I told a Thai lady that what she said was so funny that I could *die laughing*. Apparently, this was translated in the Thai language to my being seriously ill, so much so that the act of laughing would kill me. One last classic was with a Japanese woman. I was chatting with her and suspected she was using translation software, but could not be sure. Suddenly an alarm that I had set for taking medication went off. She asked me what the sound was. I said something like: *It was an alarm that I set.* The reaction was shocking. She sent me some emojis expressing shock and anger and said she does not want to talk to me anymore. Then she disappeared from the chat and blocked me. It was only after she unblocked me a few days later and I duly expressed sorrow and regret that I had the alarm go off when we were chatting, that I understood what happened. Apparently, the Japanese word for alarm is very similar to rape. The translator had translated my comment regarding setting the alarm to a statement of intent to rape, which understandably caused her to break off the chat! Although software language translators are widely used with reasonable effectiveness, one of their major weaknesses is in translating idiomatic usage. I have to ask some of my friends at Google if translators could use a dictionary of idioms similar to dictionaries for words. The idiomatic meaning should be appropriately prioritized over the individual words' meanings."

"How do you decide which woman to chat with, out of hundreds available on the sites?"

"I choose the sexy ones", said Ben and, as they both laughed out loud, they saw the elderly stewardess who was passing by their seats stop and look at Ben with a disapproving stare.

"Just joking", said Ben with a smile, addressing the remark towards the stewardess. The stewardess moved on, with a suspicious glance at both them, not really believing Ben. She did not offer them another drink just yet.

"Seriously, it is quite an art to select who you want to start chatting with. At first, I quickly eliminate what I call stupid self-descriptions or wishes for the ideal mate. Let me give you some examples of opening lines in profiles that turn me off or make me laugh: *If you are a scammer, don't contact me*, or *if you want sex, go elsewhere*, or *I am looking for a man who is smart, well educated, wealthy, healthy and will never leave me*. I remember one Chinese lady started out by saying how brilliant she was academically but because of the favoritism and bureaucracy inherent in the Chinese system, she was unable to rise to the top in China. Now that she was in the USA, she was looking for a man who would appreciate her brilliance and be with her on her presumed journey to the top. She went on to state that she does not need men for relationships or support, just appreciation of her brilliance."

Tim was laughing.

"How can she ever expect to find anybody with that self-description?".

"She is opening herself up to being exploited by unscrupulous men who would just pretend to satisfy her need for being appreciated, and there are plenty of men like that".

"I understand your elimination criteria, but then how do you actually choose who to talk to?"

Ben thought for a while and then said,

"I actually just look at their faces and if I like a face, only then do I look at what she wrote in her profile. I consider myself a good judge of people, and I start with the face and eyes as a fairly reliable indicator of a person's nature and character. If I like a face and then the profile, I would start chat. Let me add that after the first few minutes of chatting, I often stop because of something that I strongly dislike. So, there is basically a three-step elimination process, face, profile, and first few minutes of chat. If we can get beyond these three steps, we are likely to have a longer communication and get to trying to meet in person".

"Seems very logical. Can you give some examples of what you may strongly dislike in the first few minutes of chat?"

Ben thought for a while and sipped the last few drops of his drink.

"I can give you several examples. One woman berated me for being American. She was from Singapore and was not a supporter of American foreign policy. Another started asking me inquisitorial questions about my childhood experiences and current financial status. Yet another told me she did not like the fact that I was not clean shaven, and asked me about personal hygiene matters within the first couple of minutes. I couldn't possibly get along with any of these women. I quickly terminated the chats and blocked them from further communication."

"What fraction of women you screen do you actually chat with longer term?"

"I would say one out of twenty, although it could be one out of thirty, not sure because I don't keep track of such things".

"Then it must be quite boring, just trying to find someone reasonably suitable?"

Ben shook his head and smiled.

"Not at all. On the contrary, I find the process itself fascinating and entertaining. Often it is as interesting to glance through profiles, have a quick chat with someone and move on, as to chat for days with the same person. If you are a student of human behavior, as I am, you learn more about different types of people that are out there even if you reject them as relationship possibilities. There are all types of women out there, as I am sure there are all types of men. In fact, I also learn about the men on these sites by chatting with women".

"That is interesting. How so?"

"Let me give you a couple of examples. I started chatting with someone who passed my first two screens. She had a face I liked, and her profile was well written, avoiding all the obvious platitudes and wish lists. Starting the chat, I talked about myself, my interests and experiences for a few minutes. After a while, she commented: *You are such a nice gentleman. You don't talk about sex. You didn't ask me to take my clothes off on camera. Many men do that and I instantly stop talking with them!* So, you see, it was revealing to me that there are men out there who are just looking for sex talk and there must be women out there also who are willing to satisfy these men. Of course, it is possible that this was her way of inviting sex talk.

Another woman told me she was scammed by a man who she chatted with for several months and they had finally decided they should meet in person. The man said he bought an airplane ticket to visit her. She thought she was in love with him and he reciprocated her feelings. She was more excited at the prospect of meeting this guy than she had ever been with any other guy in her life. Sadly, a couple of days before he was scheduled to fly, his son fell seriously ill, and he had to cancel his plans. Then his son was diagnosed with a serious illness which needed more money than the guy said he had available. So, he asked her for money and she willingly helped him. This happened several times until a friend of hers got suspicious when she told her the story and tried to look up the guy from the personal information which he had already given her. It was not all that difficult to discover that the guy was a fake, and had scammed her for a lot of money. He disappeared when she tearfully pressed him for the truth. She had learned her lesson and apologized that she would have to do due diligence to verify me before chatting further. I offered these women a sympathetic ear and they were eager to chat and talk about their experiences, both real life and online. Even though I may not continue the conversation beyond half an hour, I found these short online chat relationships extremely informative and revelatory of human nature, particularly for cultures and societies that I would never have the privilege of coming into direct contact with. Of course, there was a type of ego thing also. Many of the women I talked with said I was one of the nicest people they had met online, Ha!"

Tim smiled, "Yes, we men can easily fall for that stuff. Did any woman attempt to scam you?"

"Yes, several times. The first one was easy to avoid, because the woman asked for money too quickly and could not answer a few probing questions I asked. The second time was much more subtle. I was chatting with this Hong Kong lady for a couple of days. Her English was quite good, since Hong Kong was a former British colony. I actually began to like her, and it seemed that she liked me too. On the third or fourth day she suddenly said that she was planning to visit a relative in Urbana, Illinois, not that far from Chicago. Her relative was an elderly aunt who was not in good health and wanted to see her niece whom she hadn't seen in years. Seemed plausible. She gave me details of her aunt's history and showed me pictures of her, a woman in her seventies. She was going to book a flight to Chicago, and if I would be so nice as to meet her at the airport and help her get on a public transport to Urbana, she would be most grateful. Seemed harmless enough, and without much risk or responsibility on my part, so I agreed. It did seem a bit coincidental that her aunt lived close to Chicago and she would be visiting her so soon after we started chatting, but I ignored the danger signs. Coincidences happen. It would be fun to meet her, and I could easily extend our meeting to a few hours or longer, depending on the circumstances. I knew the flight details and was at the airport at the scheduled time. The flight landed almost exactly on time and I got a text from her saying that she was getting off the plane and headed towards Immigration. Then Baggage Claim, and soon she would be out. I was trying to picture our first meeting in my mind. A hug for sure. A kiss? Maybe on the cheek, lightly. I did like her, so it would be easy. Also, I was considering driving her to Urbana in my car. It was a two and a half-hour drive and would give us a chance to talk and know each other better. About forty-five minutes had gone by since her text message and I was beginning to wonder why I hadn't heard from her. Was her baggage delayed? Was there some other problem at Immigration or Customs? An hour went by. Still no message. Now I was beginning to get anxious. Then suddenly there was a message from her:

Ben dear, I am so sorry to keep you waiting, but I am being detained by Customs because they found some cigars and also some food items which they say are prohibited from being brought into the US. I didn't know. I was bringing them for you as a gift. They are fining me three hundred dollars and I don't have the money with me right now. It is in my bank account which I can access tomorrow. I started crying. They said they accept PayPal. So, if you could PayPal the amount to my PayPal address, I will send them the money and pay you back from my bank account. I asked them if you can PayPal them directly, but they said they have to get the money from my PayPal account, since I am the responsible party. Sorry to cause you this trouble Ben, but please help me. It has been a long trip. I am so tired, and I am eager to meet you.

It was a no-brainer. I sent her the amount she requested by PayPal. It was a Hong Kong International transfer, but that was to be expected, since she was from Hong Kong. She was just a few feet away, stuck at Customs and soon I would be seeing her. I just hoped the PayPal would go through quickly. I thought of chastising her for not checking the restricted items lists before trying to bring cigars or other items through US Customs. The PayPal did go through, and I texted her that it did."

"What happened then?"

"Nothing! That was the last I ever heard from her. I waited some more, then texted her and found I had been blocked. The realization hit me that she was not on the flight at all. It was a scam and I was the victim. I checked with the airlines and there was no one by her name on the flight she said she was on. The text messages must have been sent, not from O'Hare but from Hong Kong or who knows where, and I was definitely out the money I had sent by PayPal. I tried to contact PayPal immediately but they could not help, because I had willingly sent the money after confirming the address and indicated that I was sending it to a friend or family. The scam had worked. The operators were probably making a lot of money from unsuspecting victims. Three hundred dollars was just the right threshold for me not to spend too much time worrying about the money or making a significant effort to catch the perpetrators of the scam and bring them to justice. The next day, I had completely gotten over it, without regrets, and continued searching for women to chat with. After this incident, I had a heightened sense of awareness, and a quickening of the pulse each time I chatted with a woman, wondering if this was another scam. Instead of being discouraged, I was enlightened, more aware, and more interested in exploring this world of online interactions. So, when the third instance happened, I was well prepared but nevertheless came very close to falling for it."

"Let's hear it".

"This time it was a Russian woman, claiming to be from St. Petersburg. She was attractive, well-educated and came across as upper-class and wealthy. That should have been a warning signal by itself. Why would someone like her even be on a dating site? Also, why would someone like her be interested in me? I actually asked her these questions directly, and she gave plausible answers. Within the first couple of days of chat, we discovered that her hobby and passion was investing in cryptocurrencies. I knew just a little about crypto, and I had some bitcoin and ether in wallets that a friend had set up for me. She was an expert and explained to me how the crypto market worked, how the whales (those who held very large portfolios of crypto) could manipulate the market and how ordinary investors like her could ride on their coat-tails and turn a profit. The trick was to figure out which way the whales would be swimming. She explained the opportunities as well as the dangers. I was an eager student and a fast learner. I wanted to try my hand at investing with her, but she would not let me because she was concerned that I would be addicted, make mistakes and lose a lot of money. I liked the fact that she had such concern for my welfare. We got to know a lot about each other's personal lives over a few days of chatting, and although we talked about dating and relationships, there was never any pressure from either side to expedite things.

I did find it odd, though, that whenever I asked to see her on video, she would be either driving or at work, and always promised *next time* with one excuse or the other. All our communication was by chat and voice messages. One day, while discussing some strategies for day-trading, I showed some acumen which she appreciated, and told me that within the short span of a week, I had come a long way from being a novice in the field. She offered to let me try my hand at trading, using her account, just to see if I had learned some basic skills and could put them to practice. I had nothing to lose, did not have to invest money of my own, and with minimal risk I could get my feet wet with day trading crypto. *Why not,* I said to myself.

It did not take long for me to click on a link and use her password and start playing around with buying and selling her cryptos. It did surprise me a bit that she would trust me enough to allow me to play with her money, but what the heck, I was smart and I had obviously impressed her! Maybe she did like me well enough and maybe I did actually have some knack for this day trading stuff. She had close to a million dollars in her account and about fifteen different cryptos in her portfolio. I was familiar with the data driven world of traders and she seemed to have access to all sorts of data for each of her cryptos. She even had an editable program embedded into her account that would recommend buy or sell actions depending on risk tolerance and short-term financial goals. She claimed that this program was highly confidential and proprietary and was the 'brain' of the company. I could edit the program to set up my own set of rules, and decide to follow them or ignore them as I choose. It took me a day or so to understand the system, and I then began trading. Many of my strategies seemed to be working. Although I lost money on some trades, I made much more than I lost and, within a week, I had been able to increase her portfolio balance by almost twelve percent, almost *one hundred grand.* It was an exciting experience to do multiple trades and use the program to predict, with a high probability of being correct, when to buy or sell or hold. After a couple of days of allowing me to trade on her account, she probably felt that I was adequately addicted. She told me that, as a reward, she would give me ten percent of what I had made for her, or ten thousand dollars. I was stunned by the offer. She said that I could set up my own account and trade my own money going forward. Their clientele was very limited and they only allowed very high net worth individuals to participate, but she could introduce me to their management and get me in. I was encouraged, happy and grateful. I had seen the program work with my own eyes and achieved some level of success to prove that my investment strategies were working.

Normally, for their clients, the initial required deposit was one hundred thousand dollars, but she could get me in for a twenty-five thousand dollars initial deposit. She would credit me with the ten thousand which she had promised me. That would leave me to put up an additional fifteen thousand to open my account. Sounded like a plan, and I agreed. It seemed that I would be foolish not to take advantage of the offer. I just had to send her my ID and a bank wire to the company for the initial deposit amount. Then I would be all set. The next day, I was all set to email her my ID and I had prepared the amount to be wired from my bank. Although I had played with the program and the trading software myself, somewhere in the back of my mind there was a warning like a blinking red light that I had not done enough due diligence before actually sending money to someone or some organization in another country. I decided to google the name of the company and the top results came up as a legitimate financial trading company based in Russia, with branches in several European cities, including St. Petersburg. Everything seemed legit. Then, as an afterthought, I decided to add the word *scam* to the name of the company and searched again. It was shocking, what I discovered! Several of the top searches were reports of people who had an experience very similar to mine, with someone asking them to first play with their money and then be tricked into sending money to open their own accounts. The women were not always from Russia. They were from different countries, and there were several women who reported these scams also, with men doing the scamming. There was a clear mention of the same company based in Russia with a warning to stay clear of doing business with them. Some of the men had sent in substantial sums of money and never heard from anyone again. I was lucky that I did the due diligence and returned from the brink of being scammed."

"What did you do next, Ben? Report her?"
"No, I decided to play along a bit and see what happens. The next day I told her that the money and ID information was ready, but some business was taking me to London the next day. So, I decided to take a detour and visit her in St. Petersburg and hand the check over directly to her or the company, whatever she preferred. It would be wonderful and exciting for us to meet in person and enjoy a few days together in St. Petersburg, I told her. We could dine at some of the restaurants she had talked about and visit some of the places in and around the city. Specifically, I wanted to visit the Hermitage Museum which we had discussed as a must-see! There was a very long silence. Then she said that she would be out of town that week, visiting a sick relative in a small village a couple of hours from the city.

Not one to give up, I said that my business in London was flexible and I could meet her after she returned, because I really liked her and was looking forward to a great relationship. When she didn't respond, I sent her a final message saying I was on to her and her scam, and I was going to report her to the authorities immediately. As expected, she went silent on me. I had no time or inclination to report her. Let others do that. I smiled to myself, and clicked on a new profile, not Russian this time."

It was time for meal service and the stewardess brought them their dinners. Tim had asked for a Bordeaux and Ben had a Merlot. They held up their glasses and toasted to 'the online dating world' and then dug into their meals in silence. The food served in the Business classes of major airlines is much better than what is available in Economy. It is usually prepared under the direction of a reputed chef who the airlines contracts with and mentions by name, in the meal-brochure available to the passengers. A sommelier is also under contract and selects the wines available, describing the history and features of the various wines in glowing terms. All of this, to create an image of exclusivity and justifying the extra cost of flying Business class. After dinner, they each ordered a dessert wine and then Tim said,

"Your stories of chatting with women are fascinating, but I would like to know how you went from chatting with multiple women online, many of whom you discovered to be fakes, to traveling all the way to Shanghai to meet a woman whom you are confident you will like enough to date seriously, and who is obviously not a fake?"

Ben was about to respond when suddenly there was an announcement from the Captain of the Boeing 787.

This is your Captain speaking. Hope you are enjoying your flight so far. We are turning the seat belt sign back on, as we are likely to encounter minor turbulence in a few minutes. Please keep your seat belts fastened and remain in your seats as much as possible. Soon we will turn off the cabin lights, and you can use the reading lights on or above your seats if you want to read. As Tim and Ben fastened their seat belts, they felt the turbulence. It was indeed mild and lasted just under a minute, and then the seat belt sign was turned off and all they could hear was the steady hum of the powerful Rolls Royce jets. Ben waited for the stewardess to clear their tables and after stowing away his retractable table top, he replied to Tim's question.

"I continued this clicking, screening, chatting, rejecting routine for several months until suddenly one day a woman's profile caught my eye. Her name is Riya. She did not claim any special talents, had a bachelor's degree in science, and was looking for a man who would appreciate her as she was and whom she could trust and rely on. Seemed very reasonable and ordinary but after reading so many overstated and childishly written profiles, this was like a breath of fresh air. She had no hesitation in talking about herself and chatting on video. Her English was poor but passable. She had a good sense of humor, and had a pleasant smile and laughed often. My dad had taught me never to trust someone who cannot laugh loudly and openly. Looking back on my many chats with various women from many different countries, and many interactions with women and men in my personal and work life, I seldom found people who could meet that criterion. Riya was a real woman with real feelings and she did not just say she liked and appreciated me, but always gave good reasons for saying and thinking so. Of course, it flattered my ego, but she did it in a way that was not too obvious. It made everything seem reasonable. She showed in-depth interest in my background, in my childhood, in my job, hobbies, and my family. She remembered small details relating to my life long after I told her. She made it seem quite automatic that we should meet and learn more about each other.

She is a college teacher and lives, not in Shanghai, but in a city called Harbin in Northern China, near its border with Russia. I had never heard of Harbin until I talked with Riya. I googled it and discovered that it is one of the coldest cities on earth and home to an Ice Festival in winter that is comparable to the more well-known one in Sapporo, Japan. Its proximity to Russia gave Harbin a unique culture that was a mix of Russian and Chinese with some of the traditions and attitudes that are more often found in countries that live through extremely cold winters. These long winters shape behavior in subtle ways. People learn to prepare for the winter, to help each other, to value the warmth of family and to be thrifty and save for a difficult day. Also, people learn to enjoy the spring and summer after a harsh winter. I will change flights in Shanghai and go to Harbin to meet her in her city".

"Wow, great!! Hope you have a good time, and finally find your soulmate".

"There is just one catch. Her family found a match for her, against her will, and wants her to marry this guy. He is also from the US, a Chinese speaking immigrant from Vietnam with his own business. Let's call him CV. Her parents believe that his Chinese speaking ability is a huge plus which she should not downplay. Riya does not like him, and feels that incompatibility cannot be overcome by a common language and conversely, compatibility overcomes the lack of a common language. I, of course, agree with her, but her family has a different view. Have to go there, talk to her and her family, and see how this plays out. I am confident that finally we will prevail."

"Well, good luck then", said Tim, yawning.

It was time to take rest. Tim was the more experienced traveler of the two, and offered Ben some advice on how to rest. Ear plugs, a Tylenol pm and an eye patch were all that he needed to get a solid five to six hours sleep before breakfast and then the arrival at Shanghai would be just a couple of hours more. Ben took his advice and they both took advantage of the flatbed with a raised partition between the two seats for privacy. They did not talk much more for the rest of the flight. As the plane began its descent into Shanghai's Pudong Airport, they exchanged phone numbers and promised to catch up back home in Chicago later that month, maybe go out for a drink or lunch. Tim knew from experience that most of the time people he met or talked with on long flights were just conversations of convenience, a way to spend time. Almost always, phone numbers and other social media contact information was exchanged but very rarely, if ever, was there any follow up. No matter how interesting the conversation, and no matter how sincerely promises were made to keep in touch, in reality it required significant mental effort to renew the casual acquaintance, and much more often than not there was no further contact.

Tim's meetings with the sales teams in China were moderately successful. They were able to turn things around at a couple of hospitals and persuaded them to buy the American product instead of its Chinese counterpart. Only time would tell if the success could be broader and sustained.

After returning home, Tim often thought of his conversation with Ben and wondered how his trip to Harbin went. However, he did not contact Ben. Almost a year passed by, until one day Tim's younger sister, who lived in Nashville, Tennessee, sent him an email saying she was finally getting married to a guy from Athens, Ohio whom she had met at an online dating site. This came as a great surprise for Tim. His sister, over the years, had convinced their family that she would never get married. Most of her close friends were women, and she had always maintained that she enjoyed her single life and did not particularly care for or seek the company of men. Their parents, and Tim also, to be honest, often wondered if she was gay. She had found this guy online and, soon after their initial contact, he had visited her in Nashville and they had hit it off from the start. That was just eight months ago, and now they were ready to tie the knot! The wonders of internet dating! Tim was reminded of Ben and wondered what had happened after his visit to Harbin, China and meeting Riya and her family. Did Riya listen to her family and get married to CV or did she start dating Ben? He decided to text Ben right away and hopefully catch up.

Ben replied to Tim's text almost immediately. They decided to meet at the bar of Theater on the Lake, a restaurant with spectacular views of Lake Michigan and the Chicago skyline after dinner the following Friday.

Tim ordered a Bordeaux and Ben reciprocated by ordering a Merlot, the same drinks they had on the flight to Shanghai. It gave a sense of bonding and continuity and memories of that long flight. After toasting to 'the online dating world' exactly the same as they had toasted on the flight, they both laughed and Tim asked Ben,

"Tell me what happened after we met last!".

"Love to tell you. Although Riya and I hit it off pretty well from the start, CV's shadow hung heavily over our meeting. The situation was somewhat complicated. Before she met me online, Riya's parents had already convinced her that CV was the best match for her and she should quickly get married to him. Riya was much closer to her mother than her father, and was afraid to go against her mother's will. On top of that, her mother was in ill health and Riya was afraid to make her upset for fear of an adverse reaction. However, after we started chatting online and after meeting with me, Riya decided that, no matter what, we were meant for each other, and she would just have to deal with her mother one way or the other.

The first time I met her parents, at the family evening meal, it was quite awkward. Here I was, looking so different, a white guy, speaking no Chinese, responding to the many comments and small talk coming my way with nothing more than a silly smile, looking pleadingly towards Riya for translation, for explanation. The meal itself was delicious. Her mother's cooking was different from and tastier than any restaurant food I had ever had. Riya's teenage son, Jin, took a liking to me since we had a common interest in science, engineering, and soccer. After the dinner was over, there was the elephant in the room relating to the logistics of where I would sleep, and whether Riya would sleep in the same room or not. Her mother said it was time to sleep, and looked at Riya and her father, and got no help from either of them. Perhaps to avoid embarrassment, they started talking about unrelated topics. Finally, her mother took the lead and set us up in an open space with a portable privacy screen acting as a space divider. She laid out two separate single mattresses on the floor, with sheets and pillows and a light comforter. These two beds were separated by about three feet, so that the unspoken protocol or propriety of our not sleeping in the same bed before we were married or at least officially dating, could be upheld. Jin would sleep in his grandparent's room.

We stayed up late that first night, lying side by side in our separate beds, talking about our lives, past and future. She was confident she could convince her mother that she should go with me instead of CV, but not so confident that she could avoid his visiting her in China, because they had been talking about it for a long time and his plans had been finalized. He would be in Harbin the following month, just a couple of weeks after I returned to Chicago. Then, after she and her family had decided how to close the issue of making a choice, she would get back to him and we would go from there. Although it was frustrating that I could not finalize everything during the visit, there was no alternative but to wait it out. Riya and I talked late into the night, in low voices, sometimes touching hands. We talked about our childhood, our parents, school, college, and past relationships. We talked about people we loved and respected and people we disliked. Our criteria for our likes and dislikes were remarkably similar. We even talked politics. The whole world was looking at the USA as a country gone mad with the emergence of Donald Trump as President and, after his Presidency was over, as a leader of the ultra-conservative minority, a minority which had recently become comparable in size with the more liberal majority. Strangely enough, most of the Chinese people that Riya knew, even in the college teacher's environment which she was a part of, seemed to support the US far-right type views. Chinese media propaganda, I found, selectively portrayed the news that supported their government's views and was not averse to promoting clearly fake news, if that would serve their purpose. Although we finally fell asleep around three am, the wake-up call came around six, and the whole town seemed to be up and getting ready to go to work. The noise of a city waking up did not allow for a lazy sleep schedule. A couple of more days of family meetings, dinners, visits to hot springs and other sightseeing and, not to mention sleepless nights, it was time for me to return to Chicago. As I said good bye to her just before the security checkpoint at Harbin's Taiping International Airport, she gave me a light kiss on my cheek. The memory of that kiss lingered all the way until I landed at Shanghai's Hongqiao Airport about three hours later. After returning to Chicago, I decided that I will contact Riya only after CV had left China. She was supposed to let me know when that happened. A month went by and I still hadn't heard from her. CV should have already left Harbin, and I was beginning to get worried. Finally, I sent her a chat message asking her how things were going. Her reply by email was totally unexpected and shocking.

Apparently, after CV arrived in Harbin, her mother was quite taken to him and insisted that Riya marry him. She also asked CV to stay on in Harbin until the matter got resolved. CV agreed, and was still around. Riya, of course, did not agree. Her mother cried and insisted for days on end and begged her to reconsider. Her health had gotten much worse and the doctor had told her to avoid mental stress. Being diabetic as well as hypertensive, stress could kill her. Riya kept hoping that she could convince her mother, but that had not happened yet and it was getting more unlikely as the days went by. Her mother was probably using her illness as a lever, but there wasn't much Riya could do about that. She was at wit's end. She was really caught between Scylla and Charybdis, and didn't know which way to go. Sleepless nights were wearing her health down. Through all this, CV didn't understand what the delay was. Neither Riya nor anyone else in her family had told him that another man was involved. He had agreed to stay on, thinking that the resolution of some obscure family matters was the cause for the delay in Riya's decision as to the timing of their marriage. She asked for my advice on how to deal with the situation.

I could think of only one solution but I wanted to think about it a bit before suggesting it to her. I told her that I would call her the following day after thinking about the situation a bit.

To me, the only reasonable solution was that she should listen to her mother, marry CV and come to the US with him. Then if she still indeed wanted to be with me instead of him, she could divorce him and come to me. That way, her mother would be able to recover her health and she could convince her mother that at least she gave her wishes a try. When I suggested this to her the next day, her first reaction was that this would not be fair to CV because CV didn't know her plan upfront. She did not think that it was right to marry with the pre-determined notion that she would divorce shortly thereafter. Of course, she was right. Then I had no choice but to sacrifice my interests completely and told her that I would be OK if we agreed that we don't know if she would divorce him or not. We would not contact each other and if she really liked him and wanted to remain married, I could live with that. She would let me know after one year one way or the other. She thought for a while and liked that solution."

Tim was silent. Ben paused. They ordered another round of drinks. The twinkling lights of the Chicago skyline were a reminder that thousands of such stories of life and love were being played out, unknown to us, unseen by us. It is only when we encounter a unique situation in our lives that we realize that it is not so unique after all and must have happened many times over the millennia of human civilization on earth. This broader perspective of non-uniqueness often helps us face the most difficult of circumstances with a confidence that a solution or a resolution can happen in many different ways as it has happened before, many times, to many different people.

Finally, Tim said, "Ben, it must have taken a lot of courage on your part to make that suggestion and give up the girl you want to spend your life with, even if temporarily".

"Not really", thinking through it carefully, did I have any other realistic option? If I had insisted, and given an ultimatum, Riya would have no choice but to say good bye to CV. Her mother would be seriously upset and who knows which direction her health would turn. If something happened to her, or even if not, it is very likely that the ill-feelings created with her mother would affect our relationship in years to come. I know of several stories where a couple got together in spite of serious objections of their in-laws, only to suffer in many different ways after their marriage. Not for me, no sir!"

"So, what happened after that?"

"I was quite prepared to wait a year, and had already started clicking on profiles, not really intending to start a new relationship, but just out of habit and curiosity, when suddenly I received a long email from Riya. We were not supposed to contact each other, so I was pretty surprised. She mentioned that she had gotten married to CV, and with the help of that documentation, she and Jin were able to get visas to accompany him back to the US. CV's home was in Los Angeles, and she had spent the first couple of weeks in learning how to get around the neighborhood and getting a driver's license. CV was the owner of a Spa and Salon and went to work every morning, returning late, after dinner. They had dinner together only a couple of times a week at most. CV had explained to her that the Spa was open until 9pm and he would usually grab a bite to eat at the Spa. Riya ate dinner by herself, but did not mind doing that, because she loved watching the ads on TV as much as following the news. Jin had enrolled in the local middle school and during his school hours, she loved going to the nearby shopping malls to do window shopping. Some days she would smell alcohol on CV's breath and wondered if he had been drinking at work, but she didn't say anything.

Then came the shock. One day CV came home just before dinner, then changed his clothes, dressed well and went out again, saying he was having dinner with an important client. Riya didn't think much of it until she realized as soon as he left that he had left his cellphone behind by mistake. She was sure he would return soon to get it. After a few minutes, there was a buzzing sound and a text message suddenly appeared on CV's phone. It said: *Hurry up honey, waiting to meet you!* There were two heart emojis and two kiss emojis at the end of the message. Riya was in a state of shock. Her brain went numb and the phone almost dropped from her hand. She did have the presence of mind to take a picture of the message with her own phone and then she put the phone back where she had originally found it. Soon after, there was a knock on the door and CV was back. Riya pretended she knew nothing and expressed surprise at CVs return. CV just said he had left his phone behind, picked it up and left. That night, he came home late, drunk and abusive. Riya ignored his behavior, and did not let on that she had seen the telling text message. She and her son slept in her son's bedroom that night behind a locked door. Riya needed to be careful. She could not be too angry or aggressive. She had applied for immigrant status based on being CV's wife. If CV chose to hurt her case, he could easily do that and Riya and her son may be deported by the US Customs and Immigration Service on flimsy say-so evidence. Riya was concerned about her son. She wanted him to continue his education in the US, rather than in China. CV definitely had the upper hand. She was asking my advice in the email as to what she should do. I was her only friend in this country and she trusted me."

"What did you advise?"

"I know nothing about immigration law, but my colleague's father is a corporate lawyer and, luckily, he was able to refer me to someone who was familiar with immigration law. He told me that as long as the marriage itself was in good faith, which it was, Riya could sue for divorce without cause. Of course, if she had evidence, like the photo of the text message, it would help her case. She could proceed on the divorce in parallel with her application for immigration status. The divorce would be automatically granted after six months. I told this to Riya and she agreed to proceed accordingly. The lawyer gave just one word of caution. It would be helpful if CV agreed to a friendly divorce. To make this happen, he advised that Riya should confront CV with the text message evidence and find out if he was having an affair with another woman and if so, would he agree to an amicable divorce? ".

"Wow, this is getting very involved. I am sure that you and Riya have to be very careful that your communications are not seen or suspected by CV".

"Yes of course, what happened after that was unexpected. One night the following week CV came home drunk again. This time Riya asked him politely if he was drinking after work. CV got very angry and accused her of trying to control his life. Riya could not restrain herself and asked him who he went out with a week ago when he also came home drunk. CV was ashen faced. *Just a client,* he stammered. *Was your client a lady who calls you honey?* Asked Riya. It was then that CV ignored the question and threatened her with divorce, and Riya quietly replied that it may be the best solution for both of them.

Riya then moved permanently to her son's bedroom, and over the next few days they continued to discuss the details of the divorce. She told CV that she would not ask him for anything as long as he agreed to a friendly divorce and assure US Immigration officials that, when they got married, they both wanted it to be much longer lasting. It was unforeseen circumstances that was prompting the divorce. The marriage itself was genuine, not one just for getting a visa, with no money exchanged as payment for the marriage. CV agreed verbally, and they proceeded to file.

Riya and Jin moved from Los Angeles to Chicago and moved in with me. The divorce would take about six to nine months to be finalized. The immigration process would take longer. Barring unforeseen circumstances, it would be completed within a couple of years. Things were going well. Riya and I were finally together and happy with each other."

It was time for a third round of drinks and a break. Tim had caught the hesitation in Ben's voice when he had said: *Things were going well...* It was as if there was a foretelling of bad things about to happen. The rest room break behind them, and with the drinks in front of them, Ben continued.

"Things were going well, Tim, until about three weeks before the divorce was to be final, Riya got a message from CV saying that he had second thoughts about the divorce and he did not think he should agree just because he was drunk one night and Riya had found a text message on his phone. Riya stood to gain a lot from the divorce and he expected some compensation from her in order to agree to tell the immigration authorities that the marriage was legitimate and not a fake one. Both Riya and I were stunned. This man had no conscience. He was asking for money to tell the truth! However, Riya's hands were tied, she was in a weak spot because she had no status in this country and had to depend on CV for getting her permanent residency status without trouble. We scratched our heads and finally decided that the best solution was that Riya would go back to Los Angeles and try to work things out amicably with CV. I did not relish the idea of her being anywhere close to CV after we had spent several months together, but there was very little choice.

Riya did not want to go. She abhorred the thought of spending time with CV again after she had assumed that it was finally all over. I pointed out that the risk of CV behaving irrationally and hurting her immigration case was one she could ill afford to take. We drafted a document for CV to sign that their marriage was in good faith and the divorce was for irreconcilable differences discovered after the marriage. Here I was in the strange situation of asking my girlfriend, and possibly future wife to go and spend time with her estranged husband to calm him down and get him to be sympathetic to her situation and hopefully sign a document that would preserve her chances for US immigration. Not to speak of the fact that earlier I had asked her to get married to this same man. What a weird combination of events and circumstances! Life has a habit of creating scenarios that make extremely unlikely situations seem believable and logical. Still, it was a very difficult decision. We planned to communicate daily by text message, and do it in a way such that CV doesn't find out. I warned Riya to be careful and avoid any possibility of physical danger. She had made some friends during her brief stay there and I asked her to keep them aware of her whereabouts at all times. Riya went off to Los Angeles, leaving Jin with me. and I was left wondering what would happen next. It was after a few uneventful days that I got a message from her that was very good news and very bad news at the same time. Can you guess what they were?"

Tim thought for a while and said,

"CV agreed to cooperate fully, but wanted money in exchange for it?"

"Nah, that would be good news and fair news. CV agreed to cooperate, and sign the document in exchange for spending a night with Riya."

Tim could not believe his ears.

"Why would he ask that? How did Riya react? How did you react?"

"I don't know for sure. Human psychology is complex. It is even more complex when it comes to how people react to broken or breaking relationships. It could be a desire for a last experience with the woman he married. It could be a revenge motive for her decision to divorce. It could be just trying to get something in return for giving her what she so badly wanted, her freedom. Who knows? Again, Riya would not even consider it because she hated him, but after some thinking I suggested that she should do whatever it takes to get him to sign the document. Of course, if she could avoid the request, that is best. In any case, I told her there was no more communication necessary on this topic between us, until she returned to Chicago. I also reminded her to be cautious about any physical danger, that's all." "Wow! What next?" was all that Tim could say.

"We had no further text exchanges for the next two days. I was obviously getting anxious, not knowing what was going on and worrying about her safety. Then on the third day, I got a message asking me to pick her up at O'Hare that night. It was such a relief!"

"Did she tell you what happened?"

"All she ever said was, *I got the document signed and I maintained my dignity and integrity.* I didn't ask her any more questions. That was three months ago. Since then, the immigration paperwork has been going through the process, with no clear idea when it would be completed, but no indication of any issues either. I have gotten much closer to her over the months than ever before and her son and I have also developed a great relationship. In fact, I have begun to think of Jin as my son. On Valentine's day, I gave her a diamond engagement ring. She was so deliriously happy!"

"Guess that ends your online quest" said Tim,

"Nah, I still click out of habit, although Riya doesn't like it. I have explained to her that it has become part of my lifestyle. She has sternly informed me that lifestyle changes are necessary. Have to bring her around"

"What a story! It is getting late and we are almost at closing time here. Let us keep in touch, and meet again for a drink or two whenever both of us are in the mood!"

"Sure", said Ben, as they shook hands and walked out of the restaurant.

The night was cold and windy, as it often is in Chicago, and the myriad twinkling lights of the city were like the stars forming a living blanket over yet another story of romance and love, similar to many others, except that this one started with a *click for romance*!

SMILE WITHOUT REASON

We created the devil – It's up to us to destroy it

The babysitter had been taking care of the toddler for over two years, and was completely trusted by the parents. She looked after the toddler as her own son. That day she did not know what suddenly came over her. The toddlers face had slowly changed before her eyes, and ended up looking like a monster's. She felt an involuntary smile on her lips and a strong urge to beat the toddler with a stick. When the toddler started crying, the next-door neighbor rushed in, saw what was going on, and restrained her physically. Then the police came and took her away, leaving the toddler in the care of the neighbor. Fortunately, the toddler was not seriously hurt. This was not an isolated incident; a global catastrophe was unfolding.

It was a Friday evening in early December in Atlanta, Georgia. It was dark, and a cold rain was falling. There was a chill in the air. Dr. Hollis Crane was soft spoken and humble, although being one of the world's top microbiologists, specializing in virology and immunology. He held senior positions both at Johns Hopkins Medical Center in Baltimore MD, and at the Center for Disease Control in Atlanta. He spent three or four days a week at the CDC and two to three days at Johns Hopkins, commuting back and forth. During graduate school at Johns Hopkins, when the world was going through the Covid crisis, he became determined to dedicate his life to learning about viruses and developing detection and cure techniques to thwart future threats to public health on a scale as massive as the Covid pandemic. That was almost fifteen years ago. This dedication had paid off as he ended up winning the Albert Lasker award, which very often precedes the award of the Nobel Prize in medicine, for providing a way to monitor the different stages of how viruses can cross the blood-brain barrier and affect the brain to cause psychiatric disorders. He still remembered how the whole world was in lockdown and individual lives as well as the economy of nations was severely affected during Covid. There was a lot of finger-pointing regarding the origin of the virus, but nothing was ever conclusively proven. It took about five years for the mutations to become rather harmless in spite of the fact that they had become immune evasive earlier. His wife, Jamie, whom he had met at graduate school was also a virologist and shared a similar passion for understanding and controlling the threats posed by new, hitherto unknown viruses. The world had been pandemic free for about fifteen years, but virologists like Hollis and his colleagues were continuing to explore new frontiers like the possible viral origins of different types of mental illness.

The human brain, and how it functions, is one of the less explored (and explorable) areas of human physiology and was yielding its secrets reluctantly but inexorably to dedicated research teams all over the world. There were several major conceptual difficulties that Hollis and his colleagues faced in their studies. First, it was impossible, practically and ethically, to study active viral processes in live human subjects. When it was possible, the responses of the subjects could not be trusted like they could be for other types of illnesses, because mental illness affected the brain itself, and the brain did not recognize that fact, a basic catch-22 situation. Mice were often used in studies because mice brains have many similarities with human brains, but there were enough differences that it was not easy to relate results from experiments with mice brains to their human counterparts.

Hollis and Jamie had two pre-teenage children, Joseph and Abigail, going to a public school in the Atlanta suburbs. They worried that their children would be overly biased towards medical science, and sought carefully to give them a broader education, with equal focus on STEM and the liberal arts. Abigail was eleven and Joseph twelve, and they were very close to each other and pretty much inseparable since childhood. Their best friends were Stan and Vicky, who lived a block away and went to the same school. Stan and Abigail were in the fifth grade while Vicky and Joseph were in the sixth. Stan and Vicky were Chinese Americans, born in Atlanta. Their father, Jason Lin, originally from mainland China, and now an American citizen, also worked at the CDC and knew Hollis both at work and as a neighbor. The Lin and Crane families were quite close and found themselves socializing and doing some things together a few times a year, with their children being the driving force behind most of their joint social activities. That Friday, as Hollis Crane drove home from work, he looked forward to the zoo trip that they had planned with the Lin family on Sunday, assuming that the weather would not stand in their way.

On the other side of the world, in an internationally well-known Institute for Virus Research, an important meeting was being held, shrouded in great secrecy. The Project X team had been formed a few years after the Covid pandemic had receded from public focus. Its mission was to genetically engineer viruses to cure illness, under the banner of what is known as Gain of Function (GOF) research.

GOF research typically involves making viruses stronger or more transmissible and could be useful for various studies including vaccine development. It has come under a lot of scrutiny by public health watchdogs because of the potential for harm to the general public if the altered virus escapes its laboratory confines. It could result in a deadly pandemic. In the US, the National Institute of Health (NIH) stopped funding GOF in 2014 and then resumed a few years later with guidelines for narrower use, stricter control and risk avoidance. Unfortunately, there has been very little international coordination or oversight relating to GOF and its control for worldwide public health risk avoidance. The Covid catastrophe should have been a clear warning that public health related to the potential for a pandemic was not a local or national issue, but of worldwide significance. Yet, in the years since, there has been no significant effort in the direction of international cooperation, and countries are still free to pursue GOF, pushing the limits of ethics and legality in their own way. The stage was set for the top-secret Project X meeting on the other side of the world.

It was a small room, with a table around which ten institute personnel were seated. The room, with no windows, was located in the most secure section of the building with multiple secret code accesses needed to reach it. All attendees wore white lab coats with a number from one through ten inscribed on the coats, with an X before the number. They were also wearing card key photo badges. The badges had their photos but no names, just the numbers X1 through X10. There was a projector at the center of the table and the person at the head of the table, with X1 emblazoned on his coat, had his laptop connected to it and seemed to be in charge of the proceedings. He started speaking in a low, barely audible voice, looking around the table:

"Welcome to our semi-annual meeting. None of you have your mobile phones with you today and this has been confirmed by our security check. There will be no recording of any type on any media and no photography permitted during this meeting. Don't worry, there will be no memory test afterwards, he said with a smile. We are being continuously monitored during the meeting and I am hoping there will be no violations of policy. Today we are welcoming a new member to our team, X4, who joined us just one week ago. This is a good opportunity for all of us to meet X4 and also summarize our mid-year status and goals going forward".

Everyone looked at X4 and nodded. X4 reciprocated with multiple nods, looking at X1 through X10 around the table. X1 continued:

"As you know, our team was formed seven years ago as a secret project with the objective of developing viruses to cure illness, with a focus on mental illness. We had seven members, and then three new members joined us three years ago. One of our members, a molecular biologist, went to an international conference last week to discuss some of our results with other world class experts in viral vector technology. His directions were to get as much information as possible, while revealing as little as possible about our work. Unfortunately, he met with an accident which I will not go into the details of, and will not be with us any longer. In his place we have a new Mr. X4, who is also an eminent molecular biologist who has worked in the same areas as the previous Mr. X4.

As you know, progress in understanding the root causes of mental illness has been excruciatingly slow because of two major reasons. The brain does not reveal its secrets easily and there are many ethical and legal issues surrounding the use of human subjects for research studies. It is paradoxical that no matter how big the potential long-term benefits, most societies do not allow the use of human subjects. Project X's goal is to fast-track progress by using human subjects in a safe way and only with the consent of the subject or their families as the case may be. Our motto is *Benefit Over Risk*. As long as this project is ongoing, and for five years after the project is terminated, only a very few people in the top echelons of our government will know the names of the people on this team, and it will remain a top secret. You don't know who each other are, and even I know you all only by your numbers and areas of expertise. This is for your own safety because the nature of your work, although altruistic, may be perceived otherwise by hostile nations or other entities. All of you have signed agreements that you will not talk about any aspect of your work outside of the walls of our institute. Not with your families, not with any colleagues outside of this group and not with any news media. Not even with any government officials. I will handle the interface with our government. This agreement must be ironclad. No exceptions. You have all been told what the penalties will be for any violations, and you know they will be enforced, with no exceptions. With that said, let us go around the table and introduce ourselves simply by our numbers and area of expertise or specialization. I will start. Mr. X1: Public Health".

They went around the table. Ms. X2: Virology; Mr. X3: Immunology; the newcomer, Mr. X4: Molecular Biology; Ms. X5: Chemistry; Mr. X6: Neurology; Mr. X7: Genetics; Mr. X8: Physics; Mr. X9: Statistics and computer modeling and finally Ms. X10: Behavioral Science.

After a round of clapping, Mr. X1 went on,

"I will summarize the progress we have made so far with our research and target group, then our current status, and finally our challenges and outlook for the next three years. Let us look at the slides now. The main focus of our work, at the request of our government, has been to cure or control aggressive behavior in humans. This will ultimately achieve the goal of reducing or eliminating violence of all types, both criminal and non-criminal. The next few slides show that we have based our work on the discovery that in mice brains (which are similar in many ways to human brains), there is a location under the hypothalamus gland, the smart control deep inside our brains, which shows very high levels of nerve cell activity when the mice are induced to be aggressive. Conversely, if the nerve cell activity is muted or stopped by altering the cells in a specific way, then the mice became much less aggressive. As you can see in this chart, aggressive behavior is reduced a hundredfold in mice after the introduction of gene alteration. We extended this idea to verify its applicability to human subjects.

We selected twenty extremely violent people from three jails. They all agreed to participate in the experiment with the promise of a large payment which will go to their families upon completion of the study. We informed them that there would be risk involved as some of our work was uncharted territory. In case they suffered adversely as a result of our studies, their families would get a handsome compensation. The twenty people are identified just by their numbers: one through twenty. You can see in the next two charts their backgrounds and history of violence and the reasons they were jailed.

Our first challenge was: how do we go inside the hypothalamus, deep inside the brain, and modify nerve cell activity there? The next three charts explain what we did. We decided to use viruses to do the job for us. Using the new technology of viral vector gene manipulation, we found a way to modify a virus, have it cross the blood brain barrier, enter the hypothalamus area and modify the DNA of specific cells in the target location. It took us over three years of experimentation to optimize the virus and the transfer process in mice. We called the modified virus VVH24 for Viral Vector Hypothalamus, number twenty-four. We were ready for our first human study.

We chose two of the most violent subjects, numbers 1 and 2 on our list and performed a baseline study of their reactions to specific stimuli for aggressive behavior. Their reactions confirmed that they were quite different from normal people with regard to aggressiveness and potential for violence, as you can see in this chart. Then we introduced, by injection, the virus targeted for the hypothalamus. If it worked as expected, then they would show a much more normal stimulus response profile compared to their baseline before the virus introduction. The next chart shows the results. As you can see here, their responses show a huge reduction in their aggressiveness and tendency for violence. Then we repeated the viral vector targeting for the other eighteen inmates. All showed positive results except for two who showed traits of *increased* aggressiveness, as you can see in this chart. This was surprising, so we decided to investigate further as to why those two subjects became more aggressive. We discovered that during the process of virus transfer between the point of injection and reaching the brain, very likely while crossing the blood-brain barrier, it changed its chemistry and instead of muting or blocking the nerve cell activity, it enhanced it, causing the increased aggression. Although this was worrisome, we felt that eighty percent effectiveness was good enough by any standards, and this therapy was workable. Although a sample size of twenty is rather small from a statistics viewpoint, this was the breakthrough we were looking for, in terms of validation of hypothesis!

We reported the results to our sponsors in the Department of Social Services who, as expected, asked us to broaden the scope of our validation. The next chart shows the two focused activity areas which we started exploring about three years ago. First, we repeated the above experiment over a much larger population. This time, instead of selecting convicts with a prior history of violence, we selected one thousand people with a non-criminal background, but all from the same ethno-religious group. As before, we informed them of the risk and reward trade-off, and gathered exactly the same baseline data before the targeted viral vector process. This time we found that seven hundred and forty people showed reduced aggressive responses, sixty were about the same and two hundred showed *greater aggression*. Although the numbers were slightly worse than the previous small sample results, they were still significant enough, statistically speaking. We continued to be worried about the twenty percent that showed increased aggression, but there was not much we could do about it. What was most worrisome was that even months after undergoing the viral vector treatment, their aggressiveness was not diminished at all. It seems the virus caused some permanent change in their brains. The second activity is more controversial but our government sponsors insisted on our pursuing it, even though I pushed back initially. We were asked to select one thousand people, equal numbers of adult males and females who were strongly religious, and do a baseline measurement of their willingness to change some of their beliefs by persuasion. We would select this group of people from a religious minority in our country. Then we would check to see if there was any change in their flexibility to change or modify their beliefs such that they were more aligned towards the majority belief structure, after the viral vector process.

Religious beliefs are the most difficult to change because they are hard-wired into our brains from birth. The hypothesis was that blocking the nerve cell activity near the hypothalamus may have some effect on the subject's willingness to change beliefs, which may be related to the reduced aggression already perceived. You can easily see why this is controversial. On behalf of our team, I got agreement from our sponsors that we will not go beyond research and proof of concept. We, as scientists, will not participate in any activity that would broaden the implementation of viral vector gene manipulation to the broader society, and specifically not be part of any attempt to actually change people's religious beliefs. In this meeting, I will not go into any discussion of ethics or legality, but just say that this was the first experiment of its type anywhere that I am aware of. Our government considers that terrorism and violence are often strongly linked to basic beliefs and the ability to alter those beliefs will benefit everyone concerned. However, our government is also fully aware that this type of experiment, and use of viral vectors to control uprisings in population subsets, is totally against international humanitarian norms. At this time, we are therefore limited to basic research validation which is what we are engaged in. If it is followed by actual implementation, other groups will be responsible for that, not us. All this activity will be obviously in total secrecy.

The next couple of charts show the startling results. Of the thousand subjects, only two would consider a change of faith before the virus intervention or *treatment*. However, after the virus treatment, five hundred and seventy four were more agreeable to consider a change of faith, two hundred were the same as before, and the remaining two hundred and twenty six became more hostile to change than they were before. This was reminiscent of the results on change of violent behavior where twenty percent actually became more aggressive. We reported these results to our sponsors about a year ago. Then we were tasked with studying *why* the twenty percent became worse. This was challenging, because we had to figure out exactly where and how the virus changed (if it did) and whether it ended up blocking the nerve cell activity in the same way in these subjects as in the majority of cases. Our results were inconclusive after two years of investigations. All we could say was that the virus, for some reason, increased the nerve cell activity instead of muting it. We do not know whether it was because the virus targeted cells in a different part of the brain or whether the virus itself underwent some changes during its traversal of the path from the insertion point in the body to the brain. We have six more months to study whether the virus itself underwent changes in the cases of the twenty percent, or just lost its way in the brain and targeted different cells than the ones intended. I have discussed the project separately with Ms. X2 and Mr. X6, our team leaders. They will work with the rest of the team on your separate assignments. We will meet again in two months to review progress.

Before we adjourn, one more reminder. All the viruses and samples we deal with here are in Risk Group 4, or RG4, which means they have the potential to cause lethal harm to the community. So, all of you must use appropriate caution and follow correct procedures for dealing with RG4 materials. No sample is ever to be removed from our premises. Any questions"?

No one had any questions. Everyone sat silently for a few minutes. Mr. X1 looked around the table, and then said" "Meeting adjourned". The members walked out of the conference room to their offices and laboratories scattered around the two storied building.

Hollis Crane did not miss too many news items in his areas of interest. He had selected the news filters that he wanted to see and every morning he would make sure that he caught the major headlines. His filters were mainly related to his research work, a few sports teams he followed, and some general science and technology news. It was the Monday morning after their family visit to the zoo with the Lin family. As he was headed to his car for the drive to work, he casually looked at the flashing news on his smartphone. A faculty member at the Wyss Institute at Harvard, working at the Laboratory for Bioengineering Research and Innovation, was arrested early that morning near his home after he smashed the window of his neighbor's car with a hammer. He did not take anything from the car. After smashing the window, he went back to his own house and back to his bed where his wife was still sleeping. The neighbors, woken up by the sound of the window glass being smashed, called police and after checking the security and surveillance cameras in the area, they had no doubt about the perpetrator of the crime, and arrested him. The police report said that he did not resist arrest, did not say anything, just smiled a strange smile, and allowed himself to be handcuffed and taken away. No motive was established. It was an unusual story - a weird, inexplicable, random act of violence. Hollis was quite familiar with the Wyss Institute and specifically the activity at the Bioengineering Research Lab because they were doing work in novel drug delivery methods which closely paralleled his own work at Johns Hopkins and the CDC. He made a mental note to find out any updates to this intriguing story. His day was busy as usual and the news item of the morning was far from his mind as he went through several long meetings which were commonplace for Mondays. These meetings were meant to review the progress of the previous week and set directions for the team for the rest of the week. As the last meeting was nearing its end, he looked at his phone and let out a clearly audible,

"Oh My God!" so that everyone paused and looked at him. Embarrassed, Hollis just said "Sorry", and walked out of the room and went straight to the nearest common room. Then he read the flashing headlines again, disbelievingly. A day earlier, a faculty member at the National Institute of Virology in Pune, India was arrested for throwing hot coffee in the face of a Starbucks employee for no obvious reason. Bystanders said that the Starbucks cashier had asked him if he wanted anything else besides the coffee, which apparently drew this bizarre response. His family and colleagues told police that he was never disposed to violence, had no argument or fight with anyone in recent memory, and was known as a serious self-effacing academic in his work environment. In addition, he was a loving father and husband. It was just completely out of character, an absolutely crazy and unbelievable act, according to the news report. Hollis instinctively felt that there could be a connection between the two incidents, in spite of their being on separate continents. It was difficult to assume coincidence when both the Harvard and Pune incidents had a couple of key things in common – faculty members at institutes engaged in biological research. Hollis went back to the meeting room and sat through the rest of the meeting, but his mind was not there. He was thinking about how to get additional information on the two incidents and also wondered if there was any way he could find out what they were working on in their laboratories at the time. That evening, as soon as he had finished dinner, he started searching the news networks for any information or updates. There was nothing. He decided to call Jason and ask him if he was aware of these two incidents. Jason didn't pick up the phone call, so Hollis decided to catch him the next day at work.

Jason had not yet read or heard about the two incidents involving members of the Wyss Institute at Harvard and the National Institute of Virology in Pune, when Hollis walked into his office the next morning. When Hollis told him about the news items, Jason's face turned ashen. Hollis sensed that Jason knew something pertaining to these incidents. Jason didn't say anything for a few seconds then asked "Do you know the names of these two people who were arrested - one in Boston and the other in Pune?"

"No, I couldn't find the names anywhere in the news feeds, but it shouldn't be too difficult to find out who the Wyss Institute guy was. I know several Department members there".

"The reason I am asking", said Jason, "is that about ten days ago I attended an international conference on viral vector technology in Glasgow, Scotland".

"Oh, yes, I know about that conference. I was planning to attend too, but canceled at the last minute" interrupted Hollis. Jason continued:

"At this conference, one of the attendees, I believe from somewhere in Asia, was involved in an automobile accident on an icy road near the conference location. He stumbled in to the conference center, with blood dripping from his face and upper body, was helped by several conference attendees to lay down on a couch in the lobby, and attended to by other staff at the conference before he became unconscious and they called an ambulance to take him away to a nearby Hospital Emergency.

He did not recover in time to attend the conference but I heard through the grapevine that he was carrying a vial of an experimental virus culture with him when the accident occurred. No one knew anything about the vial or what it contained, and no one thought much about it until after the accident. Since he was not in a condition to talk or respond to questions before the conference ended, no one ever knew the details of his intended contribution to the conference. Every conference requires attendees to submit abstracts of their proposed talks or discussion items, but these are very brief and in summary form, so it was not possible, from his abstract, to figure out what exactly he was planning to speak about. I would not remember this incident were it not for the fact that out of over three hundred attendees at the conference, several were from the Wyss Institute and the National Institute of Virology in Pune at my dinner table one evening. I have their business cards and want to check if the people involved were someone I might have met. However, in the broader sense, do you see what I am getting at? *Is it possible that the vial he was carrying was broken or damaged somehow in the accident and some conference attendees were exposed to it?* Even if that were the case, I know of no virus or agent that could cause a behavior change leading to sudden aggressiveness or violence as in these two cases."

Hollis and Jason sat quietly looking at each other for a minute or so before Hollis asked,

"Can you try to find out more about the guy who was involved in the accident? Is he recovered enough now? Is he still in Glasgow? Can he share with us the contents of the vial he was carrying? Where is the vial now? etc. On my side, I will try to find out the names of the two people who were arrested".

With that Hollis returned to his office to start another busy day. There was unease at the back of his mind, very strong unease.

"I have called this emergency session to inform you of some news that pertains to our work", said Mr. X1 at the hastily called meeting just a few days after their last meeting, where Mr. X4 was introduced as a new member.

"Our government does not allow easy access to all international news, so I believe that most of you have not heard about the strange incidents involving several attendees at the International Conference on Viral Vector

Technology at Glasgow a few weeks ago. Also, I have not given you all the details regarding one of our team members, the former Mr. X4 who I mentioned went to an international conference and was involved in an accident, and is no longer with us. I owe you a more complete story, which I now have the permission of our government to relate to you, in the strictest confidence. Mr. X4, the previous one that is, went to the conference in Glasgow, Scotland to discuss some highly technical aspects of gene modification with some of the world's leading experts. Unknown to any of us, without permission, and in clear violation of our rules, Mr. X4 took with him a vial of the virus which we had modified for the experiments I had described to you previously. We discovered this during a routine inventory count of vials. It took us several days to confirm that one vial was missing. We were about to contact him urgently in Glasgow when we found out that he had met with a traffic accident while he was presumably carrying the vial with him to the first day of the conference. He was unconscious for a week in a Glasgow hospital and then fell into a coma from which he still has not recovered. *We have no idea what happened to the vial.* All our vials are made of glass, so if it was on his body at the time of the accident, it may very well have been crushed and broken, and the virus could have escaped. We were waiting for him to recover from the coma to determine where the vial was or what may have happened to it, when we were alerted to three incidents that have occurred in the past two days involving attendees at the conference.

One of these was a random aggressive act by a faculty member at the Wyss Institute in Cambridge, Massachusetts. The other was also a random aggressive act by a faculty member at the Institute of Virology in Pune, India, and the third was by a hospital worker in Glasgow at the hospital where X4 was admitted. This hospital worker, a nurse assistant, hit a patient with one of his shoes when the patient asked for water. He has been put on leave and is under observation. All these three people were in close contact with X4 after his accident and I believe it is a very likely possibility that the virus escaped the vial and infected their brains. They are probably victims of the same deviant behavior like the twenty percent who show greater aggressiveness under the influence of the modified viral vector. This is a cause for serious alarm, because we do not know much about this modified virus VV-H24. We don't know how rapidly it can be transmitted, its modes of transmission, and its mutation properties. We don't know any antidotes. Given its potential for harm, we have decided to redirect our team's mission. We need to understand its mode of transmission and try to discover antidotes, or ways to reduce the efficacy of the virus. This re-direction is effective immediately. Also, this work has to be carried out in extreme secrecy because all of us, all of you, are in grave risk of international reprisals if it is found out that the virus escaped from our institute, even though it was the work of one rogue member. If no questions, let us meet in one week and review our progress".

There were no questions, and the team dispersed.

Hollis Crane was a determined man. He had risen to the top of his profession because of a combination of skills, the most relevant of them being the ability to synthesize knowledge from diverse areas of science and technology and apply them in a multidisciplinary setting. This is an incredible asset for new developments in molecular biology and virology. There is considerable similarity with detective work where clues are all important and intelligently pursuing them can lead to success. Dead ends have to be foreseen and avoided early. After several calls to professional colleagues all over the world, Hollis and Jason had figured out that both the scientists who were arrested had attended the Glasgow conference. They also found out about the Asian scientist who was in a coma after an automobile accident and the Glasgow hospital worker who was under observation in a mental ward. Hollis asked Jason if he knew anything about the Asian scientist. Jason replied in the negative, but Hollis persisted. Since Jason was originally from China, and possibly had connections in the Asian world, Hollis asked him to try to find out more about the background of the man, if he could. Jason said he would try. Hollis was thinking that it was possible that all three of the affected people may have been exposed to some sort of unknown drug or pathogen that had affected their behavior and made them irrationally aggressive. Although he knew of no agent that could have such a specific behavioral impact, he went to bed that night planning to ask several of his colleagues if, during the course of their research activities, they had come across any agent that could be remotely linked to such behavior change, in humans or animals.

Next morning, all hell broke loose. News media all over the world began reporting very similar strange cases of sudden onsets of super-aggressive behavior by previously normal people. The behavior was often violent and irrational enough to cause serious physical injury to others. In some cases, the person injured became violent himself later, as if he had caught the 'violence-bug' as the media named the episodes. There were no precursors, no warnings before the virus struck. In the case of Covid, the disease progressed slowly starting with coughs or fever or sore throat or loss of taste and smell. Not so with this bug - no warning signs, a sudden act of violence, followed by forcible restraint and removal from the public environment. The only possible warning sign was multiple reports of the aggressor smiling strangely without cause, shortly before turning violent. There were twenty-five cases in the Boston area, seventeen in New York and four in Houston. There were fourteen cases in Glasgow and eleven in the London area, one hundred and twelve in India, and forty-four in Japan. All within two days. The public health services of the countries involved ordered shelter in place until further notice and urged the population to minimize exposure to strangers. Lockdowns and masks were being considered. It was reminiscent of the Covid pandemic over a decade ago, but scarier, because this, whatever it was, seemed to be affecting the brain and causing bizarre changes in behavior, and it appeared to be highly transmissible. Sane people were turning into lunatics. It was a disaster and a potential catastrophe on a mind-boggling scale.

Hollis, through one of his professional contacts in India, had found out that there was some discussion in a previous conference three years ago on how the hypothalamus area in the brain affects the aggression level in mice. Also, through one of his contacts at the Wyss Institute, he became aware of some European gene modification viral vector work that was done to try to alter the brain activity in mice. However, when he looked up the details of that study, it was clear that the modified virus would not work because it was not able to enter the brain of the mice. The conclusion of the study was that further modification work was needed for the virus to be able to cross the blood brain barrier and be effective in its intended purpose. Hollis wondered if *someone had done that work and not talked about it* in the open literature.

The CDC and several national disease control centers in the UK, India and the US began studying samples of blood, saliva and tissue from the affected people. The hospital and public health workers started using very strict protective measures, wearing Level-A Personal Protective Equipment (PPE) that is expected to guard against skin, eye and respiratory exposures. Both Hollis and Jason were close to this activity at the CDC although they were not involved in the actual sample analysis which was done by the technicians. Within a few days the scientists had identified the virus responsible. It was an AAV (adeno-associated virus) type of virus that was modified to alter the DNA of the target cells. Although AAV based gene therapy was well known, and some drugs approved already, it was clear that the protein component of the specific virus with the modified AAV had *never been seen before*. Scientists named the new virus AAV-Mod3, and the disease AA-Vid32. It was almost exactly thirteen years since Covid-19. Whether the virus was newly man made or a mutated form of what existed before was not obvious and needed further analysis. *Who was patient zero? How did he come into contact with the virus? What was the incubation period?* There were many unknowns.

Within a few days, the number of cases worldwide had gone from a few hundred to several tens of thousands, with an alarmingly accelerating rate. The PPE that the doctors and lab technicians were wearing seemed to be only partially effective, and there were several cases where the virus penetrated the PPE and victimized those in the health care business. An effort had started to make the PPE less porous. In the case of Covid, many people recovered fully and older people were at higher risk of death. In the case of AA-Vid32, no one died, but no one had recovered either, at least not till now. They remained strangely aggressive and violent and had to be kept under close supervision at all times. There were reports of people hurting themselves by being violent even when under restraint. This began straining resources. Hospital facilities, including mental illness wards, were not used to the sudden influx of people who needed to be restrained and monitored. A whole new support system needed to be set up, similar in some ways to the world reaction to Covid infections. Public health authorities were asking family members to lock those affected at home, instead of straining the hospital and mental care system. Prescription tranquilizers were the only medication that was being administered, and they were not working all that well. Tests were still to be developed and vaccine work needed to start. The virus seemed to be far more transmissible than the SARS-CoV-2.

The CDC was aware that AA-Vid32 was fundamentally more insidious and deadly than Covid or any other virus that had previously attacked mankind. Previously, people's brains were unaffected. So, they protected others as well as themselves when they fell ill. They were able to seek care and voluntarily isolate themselves. In the case of AA-Vid32, the brain itself was affected. People did not realize they were ill. So, they could not and did not seek care or protect others from catching the infection. The suddenness of the onset of aggression made it difficult to thwart or mitigate the effects of the violence. Its unique to mental illness that people don't realize they are ill, and this probably contributed to the much higher transmissibility of AA-Vid32 compared to Covid.

Hollis and Jason and their teams at CDC, Johns Hopkins and other laboratories were working around the clock to find out more about the virus and approaches to develop a vaccine and a cure. The *smile before the onset of aggressive behavior* was a clue that Hollis did not ignore. He remembered how his brother, Albert, when he first came down with schizophrenia, would sometimes smile or even laugh when he heard voices in his head. The virus probably first affected the cingulate cortex, a part of the brain that controlled emotions like smiles and laughter, and possibly also behavior. He urged the virus detectives to check if the structure of the virus enabled it to selectively attack the cingulate cortex. Although previous literature discussed behavior changes in mice by targeting the area near the hypothalamus gland, the evidence of the smile as a precursor indicated the virus was actually targeting the cingulate cortex in humans.

Before going to bed every night, Hollis pored over research papers on viral vector gene therapy, focusing on those that targeted the cingulate cortex. He was searching for any clue that would give him some idea of what the key modification was and how it was done. Only then could scientists begin to figure out antidotes and vaccines. The more he read, the more he began to suspect that someone somewhere had done the virus modification in a laboratory with the objective of affecting behavior. The accident in Glasgow that had injured the Asian participant could very well be related to the virus being accidentally released and affecting the first three people a couple of weeks ago. It would be difficult to prove anything, but the proverbial genie was out of the bottle, and the focus now had to be containment and cure.

While Hollis was focusing on understanding how the virus had entered the brain and which part of the brain was first attacked, Jason was working with his team on containment and cure. There were many studies done during the Covid years on mask effectiveness with different types of masks, as well as the benefits of social distancing. The size of the AAV-Mod3 virus was in the same ball park as the SARS-CoV2, around *one-tenth* of a micrometer, so the same scientific basis for wearing masks should apply.

The difference lay in AAV-Mod3 being more inclined to be freely floating by itself in air instead of being attached to water particles. Thus, masks were a lot less effective since the pore sizes of the masks was around *three-tenth* of a micrometer. Masks were more effective for SARS-CoV2 because the viruses were more often attached to much larger water particles, instead of being free-floating, and therefore were blocked by the pores of the mask.

That morning, Hollis was at work when his desk phone rang and at the same time his secretary knocked on his door and entered without being let in. She signaled to him to pick up his phone. It was a call from the office of the Secretary of Defense, inviting Hollis to attend an emergency meeting of the National Security Council at the White House in the afternoon. Hollis had to get on a flight in one hour and would be picked up at Dulles airport by the Security Council staff and driven to the White House. Wearing N95 masks would be mandatory at the meeting. Hollis was one of three virus experts requested to attend. The meeting was attended by the usual members of the Security Council, including the Vice President. The President had delegated authority to his Vice President for all matters related to this topic. This was the second time for Hollis to be at the White House. The first time was a recognition dinner in honor of his winning the Lasker Award, together with thirty other American Lasker Award and Nobel prize winners who were also invited guests of the President and First Lady. The meeting was chaired by the Secretary of Defense who started the proceedings by reminding everyone of the sudden worldwide emergence of the AAV-Mod3 virus and its effect on its victim's behavior.

He asked Hollis and his colleagues to verbally summarize everything they knew about the virus and its mode of transmission. This they did, and then they were thanked for their contribution to the meeting and asked to remain silent and observe the rest of the meeting, but be prepared to answer further questions when asked. Hollis thought the protocol was interesting, but was happy to comply. The Secretary of Defense continued:

"We are gathered here today to discuss our possible courses of action in case senior members of our government, including myself, the Vice President or the President himself gets infected with AAV-Mod3.

As you have just heard from the virus experts, this situation is unprecedented in our history, and in fact in the history of humanity. It has never before happened that the leader of any country has the potential to suddenly go crazy and do something to damage the self-interests of his country, including starting a war. Our back-up systems and processes are geared towards addressing illness, death, and even insanity, but not sudden insanity. As you heard from the experts, there is no warning, no precursor. Let's say we suspect that our President has become infected, and he starts acting strangely. We currently have no legal process to immediately remove him from the control of our key assets, including the control of the nuclear button. Our goal here is to define such a process, quickly, as best as we can. You heard from Dr. Crane that the only warning we may get is that the affected person has a strange smile, without any cause, before turning violent and aggressive. We do not know how reliable an indicator this is, but it is all we have to go on."

The Secretary of the Treasury spoke up:

"We need to define *strange smile* more precisely before we can act on it."

"Correct", replied the Secretary of Defense.

"Perhaps we can agree that we will monitor closely anyone who smiles without cause, preparing to restrict his or her actions at a moment's notice if aberrant behavior exhibits itself. This is such a weird and difficult discussion that we are having here. However, such is the nature of illnesses that affect the brain. People cannot be trusted to take care of themselves. They become different people. Their brain is essentially gone. My suggestion is that all government officials agree, by signing a document which we will draft quickly, that they may be forcefully restrained and monitored if they exhibit the symptoms of being infected with the AAV virus. Currently, a smile without cause is the only symptom we know. More may be added later. We will ask all non-government organizations, public and private, to follow similar guidelines. This is a quite different situation from the Covid experience which we faced over a decade ago. We never had to physically do anything against someone's will. Mental illness or crazy behavior was not involved then. It is now. If any of you can think of a better approach to reduce risks to our national security from the impact of this virus, please speak up now. If I do not hear any 'nays', please raise your hands in agreement. My plan is to implement the above order within the next few hours, certainly before the end of the day. We cannot afford to wait." Everyone in the room raised their hands. The Secretary's plan of action seemed reasonable. Of course, even with the signed consent, the legality of the action was somewhat questionable, but no one could think of a more practical solution. Restrain someone who acts or is about to act crazily and may hurt someone, seemed the right thing to do.

Suddenly Hollis froze. His heart started thumping loudly and he felt sweat break out on his forehead. He had detected the slightest of smiles quivering on the corner of the lips of the Secretary of Defense. It was out of context. Totally. The smile broadened a bit. The whole room froze as they looked at him. The Secretary of State looked at the Vice President and they nodded at each other. They made eye contact with the security guards near the doorway, who walked in and stood on either side of the Secretary of Defense, who looked at them with a puzzled expression, his hand still raised above his head, signaling his vote for his plan which was about to be dramatically implemented right then. He suddenly jerked his hand downwards and started running towards the door. The security guards grabbed him, one on each arm and led him away, out of the room. The Secretary of State, visibly shaking, stood up and adjourned the meeting. Hollis was thinking that they had all been in the same room as the Secretary of Defense. Were the N95s really effective? Who knew? Who may be next?

The news of the Secretary of Defense succumbing to the virus spread through the hallways of DC like wildfire. He was the first high ranking government official to be infected. Could the President be next? Rumors and speculations were flying. There were similar stories of public as well as private officials in other countries having to be forcibly restrained and locked up. There were stories of people being injured – by knives, sticks, stones, bottles, bare hands, basically anything that can be wielded or thrown. Guns had been involved. Children were being hurt by their parents, parents by children, students by teachers, teachers by students; workers at factories were pushing co-workers into running machinery, endangering lives, sometimes costing lives. It was just two and a half weeks since the first episodes, and there were well over seventy thousand cases worldwide.

Mr. X1 called the team meeting to order and started without mincing words.

"There are now close to one hundred thousand cases worldwide with no end in sight. Remember that our initial data showed eighty percent of the subjects had less aggressive behavior after virus treatment, and only twenty percent had deviant higher level of aggression. The actual data worldwide seems to show a much higher percentage for the deviant behavior. It seems that the virus is working in a different way than we had intended, and we do not know why. Also, there are numerous reports of people having a strange smile for no reason before becoming aggressive. The most high-profile case with this symptom was the United States Secretary of Defense who had to be escorted from a meeting yesterday after exhibiting the smile symptom. It's been a week since our last meeting and I am looking for a progress report on mode of transmission and possible antidotes. Who will go first?".

Ms. X2 the virologist led off:

"Judging by the smile syndrome, it seems that the virus is attacking the cingulate cortex, rather than the hypothalamus area as we had originally targeted. To me that indicates one of the modified proteins is binding differently to the vector virus. I need some more time to replicate the viral vector targeting the cingulate cortex instead of the hypothalamus."

Mr. X3, the immunologist went next.

"X4, X5, X9 and I have been working on the mode of transmission of our virus. In our early experiments we injected it into our subjects for direct and quick effect without studying the detailed transmissibility characteristics. It now appears that the virus can be transmitted through air and can actually have a different attack route and target when it enters the subject via the airborne route rather than being injected into the bloodstream".

X1 interrupted:

"That is a remarkably interesting comment and may explain why the virus seems to attack the cingulate cortex rather than the hypothalamus. It could be explained by the different pathway to the brain. Possibly there is some sort of difference in virus mutation or targeting based on airborne inhalation versus injection into the blood stream?"

"Yes, possibly", said X3. "We need to investigate further".

X1 asked:

"Any update on antidotes? How do we neutralize this virus?"

X4, the molecular biologist, replied:

"We have tried several approaches with multiple anti-viral cocktails, but no success so far. The basic problem is that the virus targets the brain and the anti-viral cocktails we are working with are not good at penetrating into the brain. Further update at the next meeting."

X1 looked around the table. No one else had anything further to report.

"Meeting adjourned till next week".

Hollis was planning to visit his brother Albert in Toronto during Christmas for a family get together, but given the state of affairs, all travel plans had to be canceled or indefinitely postponed. Airlines had already canceled all international flights and maintained only a skeleton system of domestic flights. Passengers who were doing emergency travel were wearing hazmat suits on all flights. Albert had severe mental illness from the relatively young age of 24. He was diagnosed with psychosis and schizophrenia. It took several episodes over three or four years to be properly diagnosed, and it took another couple of years for the doctors and psychiatrists to agree on the right medication and dosage that would keep him stable, and the schizophrenia in control. Albert had a caretaker, Janice, appointed by Hollis, and Hollis maintained regular contact with Albert as well as Janice for support as well as monitoring purposes.

Hollis and Albert were very close before Albert's illness manifested itself, before Albert became hostile and introverted. The family did not know that it was schizophrenia at that time. It was only much later, after many serious and severe episodes, some involving police, that Hollis realized that Albert was lost to him forever as a normal brother. At best, his schizophrenia would be partially under control, but never go away completely. Hollis was quite familiar with the medications Albert was taking. The medications prescribed for Albert were a new type of schizophrenia medication, known as fourth generation atypical antipsychotics. Few psychiatrists prescribed this medication, but they did so for Albert because most of the other conventional antipsychotic medications did not work for him. Hollis had helped Albert get a prescription for these medications and Hollis had permission from Albert to stock up on them and send Janice two month's supply at a time. He always kept about a year's supply on hand. Hollis made sure, through frequent phone calls with his brother as well as Janice, that Albert was taking the medications every day as prescribed. However, schizophrenics are notorious for stopping their medications when they felt fine, failing to recognize that they were fine only because of the medications. Janice had the important task of making sure Albert took his daily dose. It was mid-afternoon and Hollis called his brother from work and explained why his Christmas visit plans had to be canceled. Albert just said "OK" and hung up. Hollis was a bit taken aback by the curt response but nothing was unexpected when it came to Albert's behavior, even when he was taking his medication. He made another call, this time to Janice, and reminded her that the AAV virus was wreaking havoc and to be careful not to unduly risk exposure to the virus. Also, he alerted her to the symptom, the smile without cause. After finishing the calls, just as he was about to get back to his email, there was a knock on his door and Jason rushed in.

"Hollis, Vicky...Vicky..."

"What happened to Vicky?"

Hollis stood up from his chair and walked over to Jason, but stopped before getting too close.

"She has it." Jason was close to incoherent.

"My wife saw the smile, and Vicky was playing with a knife in the kitchen. When she approached Vicky to take the knife away, Vicky attacked her and nicked her forearm. My wife was able to grab the knife from her and tie her hands together and lock her up in her room. Vicky, my Vicky.... she is on tranquilizers. Maybe I passed it on to her, although I am without any symptoms since returning from Glasgow".

Jason slumped down on a chair and held his head in his hands, and sobbed uncontrollably. Hollis didn't know what to say. Wiping his eyes with the cuff of his shirt, Jason continued,

"I went out drinking with a group of scientists one evening in Glasgow and a researcher from Asia, when he was drinking, talked about some super-secret work on viral vectors being applied to change behavior in humans, that he had heard about from a fellow scientist. It seemed third hand, so I didn't pay much attention. I wonder if the work is real and it relates to the AAV that is spreading here. I have to try and contact that fellow and see if I can get any more information. I just hope I can get my Vicky back."

Hollis was scared, deeply scared. He had never had such a helpless feeling any time before in his life. No one who had contracted the virus so far had recovered. The recovery period, if any, was totally unknown. The danger was now so close to home. Vicky and Stan hung out frequently with Joseph and Abigail. Could his kids be the next victims? Science and detective work had to move fast. How the virus combined with the cells in the brain must be elucidated. Antidotes must be found. If everyone succumbed to the virus, there would be no one left to restrain anyone, no one left to find an antidote, no one left who was sane. Humanity would have self-destructed without nuclear annihilation, climate change, or being hit by a killer asteroid.

It was the third week after the first patient in Scotland fell victim. The worldwide case count had reached close to half a million. This was in spite of extreme steps that all countries were taking to prevent spreading the virus. Masks, PPE, social isolation, lockdowns, and lock-ups of those affected, were all being strictly followed. This time there was no partisan political sides being taken by anti-maskers. There were no anti-maskers. There were no anti-vaxxers either, but that was perhaps because there was no vaccine developed yet. All parties were preaching the same gospel: let us go overboard to protect ourselves. People who had never prayed before were praying to whatever gods they could think of. They were much more scared of AAV than they were of the SARS-CoV-2 virus. There is something about losing your mind that is much more frightening than any physical illness. Someone could be the community leader for virus response one day and succumb to the virus only to be locked up the next. There was panic in the air, in every community, every town, every country and every continent.

Mr. X1 called the meeting to order. Everyone was wearing their hazmat PPE suits. One seat was empty. X10 was missing. X1 began speaking in his usual low voice,

"Sadly, as you know, two days ago Mr. X10 fell victim to the virus while doing some experiments. We do not know whether he was careless or if it was in spite of his taking all precautions. The other team members have locked him up in a room and removed anything that he may use to hurt himself. He keeps asking to be let out and allowed to go home to his family, but obviously we cannot do that. Anyway, who will give us the progress report for last week's activities?"

X4, the molecular biologist, raised his hand.

"I will. Several of us worked on two different areas. Let me quickly summarize the results on behalf of everyone involved."

Most of the other attendees nodded in assent, and it was clear that X4, although new to the group, had assumed a leadership role.

"We found that a commonly used tranquilizer reduced the aggressive behavior for a period of time, but unfortunately the behavior resurfaced once the effects of the tranquilizer wore off, usually within a day. X10 is currently on this tranquilizer and seems to be doing OK. More work needs to be done to figure out how the tranquilizer works in the brain, so that we could modify it to increase its effectiveness and hopefully make it permanent instead of temporary, but this would take time and it has to be a much bigger effort than our team can handle. A few of our subjects have schizophrenic tendencies and take medications to control their schizophrenia. We are studying how our virus interacts with this medication. We are also studying the incubation period in the same human base population that we did the original study on, using airborne viruses instead of injections. It seems that over seventy percent of those who had previously been positively affected (reduced aggression) by the injected virus were now negatively affected (became more aggressive) when they were exposed to the airborne virus. The incubation period averaged forty-eight hours, the earliest being around twenty-four hours. This is probably the basic reason why we see such a dramatic increase in worldwide cases. Clearly, *the airborne virus acts in a different way from the injected virus*. Also, the airborne virus seems to be highly transmissible, while our experience with the injected virus was the opposite."

X1 was impressed and said so.

"Good progress, team. Although the virus may have started its journey right here, hopefully we can find a way to stop its progress right here too."

With that X1 adjourned the meeting until the following week.

Jason had finally tracked down the researcher he had drinks with in Glasgow. He was in Guangzhou. He told Jason that one of his wife's relatives was working on a top-secret project involving viruses but there was no way he could get any information because all information flow was strictly under government control. Jason pleaded with him, saying that his own daughter was stricken, and he would like to know if any member of that special project knew anything about cures or antidotes, since they had probably a head start in understanding and controlling the AAV virus. If he could just get that information, Jason would be grateful. The researcher said he would try, but no promises.

Everyone had set up a mutual monitoring network. Hollis had asked his wife, Jamie, to closely monitor Joseph and Abigail. He would monitor Jamie. Jamie would monitor him at home. He and Jason would monitor each other at work. The out-of-context smile was the only tangible precursor they could rely on. It was just after lunch, three days after Vicky got infected. Hollis had just returned to his office when his phone rang. Hollis recognized the caller-ID as Janice, his brother's caretaker. Her voice was anxious and scared. Albert had gotten infected, probably because he had ventured outside, ignoring the proper protocols for wearing his protective suit and mask. He had become aggressive and violent towards her. Janice had run out of the house, sought a neighbors help and was able to tie his hands and lock him in one room. There is a crazy look in his eyes, Janice told Hollis. Both Janice and the neighbor who helped were wearing their hazmat suits so the chances were that they would escape infection. Hollis asked if Albert was taking his medications regularly. Janice replied that until he came down with the virus, he was, but after he turned violent and was locked up, she had not had a chance to give him the medication. He was on tranquilizers instead. She would try within the next couple of days to give him his regular medication and update Hollis. Hollis wished her well and hung up. As if his brother's schizophrenia was not enough, now he had to deal with his AAV infection. Hollis spent the rest of the day working on reading and analyzing the hundreds of reports, statistics, results of experiments with viruses from different laboratories all over the world and other related data that filtered in to his desktop. Very few people visited him at his office. Everyone was avoiding or minimizing contact with others.

Jason walked into his office late in the day and said that his Asian researcher had found out from his contact in the secret project that some anti-depressants could temporarily alleviate the symptoms. This was similar to the results that the CDC was already aware of. It was late in the day. Hollis leaned back in his chair, looked at the dull grey late afternoon sky through his office window and wondered whether the virus would wreak havoc then disappear, like the flu or SARS-Cov2, or remain among us indefinitely. He wondered what the incubation period was, or whether the virus would shortly mutate to either a deadlier or hopefully less deadly version. Efforts to discover a vaccine had just started. He wondered how long that would take, and whether the development work could be fast-tracked. The m-RNA vaccines developed for Covid were released too soon, it was discovered later. The Covid variants were vaccine evasive, so the vaccines had lost their effectiveness, but the side effects damage was done. One had to me more careful this time around. No one had any definitive answers. He locked his desk, left his office, locked the door behind him and walked slowly towards his car in the far corner of the parking lot.

There was excitement in Mr. X1's voice as he called the emergency session to order.

"I have some good news to report finally", he said.

Then he looked at Mr. X4 and asked him to describe the progress since the previous meeting. X4 spoke in a steady and unemotional tone:

"I am making this report on behalf of all our team members who have entrusted me to summarize the data in this meeting. In our experimental pool of subjects, we have about three hundred who became more aggressive after the viral vector injection. We have an additional one hundred who have become infected with the airborne version of our virus. Three out of these four hundred or so subjects were on antipsychotic medication before the tests as a result of being diagnosed with psychosis and schizophrenia years ago. When they were given their routine schizophrenia medications after the onset of their aggression, we were surprised to discover that all symptoms of their aggression disappeared. When we suspended the medication, their aggressive behavior did not relapse, although their schizophrenia did. We believe that somehow the blocking of the neurotransmitters in the brain, which is what the antipsychotic medications do, also reduces the nerve cell activity that triggers aggression. Then we repeated this over a much larger population of over two thousand affected people, and in over ninety five percent of the cases, the aggressive behavior disappeared. Finally, and this is also good news, we have discovered two different mutations, both milder, and in both cases, the antipsychotics for schizophrenia work."

As X4 took his seat, the team members stood and clapped for a long time. X1 spoke again:

"We have asked our government to quickly release to the whole world the information that atypical antipsychotic medication, normally given for schizophrenia, could be used to eliminate or significantly reduce the symptoms of AAV affliction. Although we cannot share the detailed back-up data without revealing our use of human subjects, we feel we cannot sit on this information for even one hour, in all good conscience. Our government sponsors just got back to me, agreeing with my proposal. We were asked to continue our work and wrap up the loose ends of our study. By now, all major public health centers in the world have received the information. It is also on our government website, with all due disclaimers. If there are no other questions, let us all get back and complete our work for the day, summarizing the data and our conclusions. Meeting adjourned."

Hollis knew from his experience with his brother's medications that many early medications for schizophrenia were in fact closely related to anti-depressants. The latest atypical antipsychotics worked on neurotransmitters like dopamine and serotonin in the human brain and blocked or changed the intercommunication between different parts of the brain. This helped schizophrenics lead close to normal lives. Although a lot of progress had been made in the last twenty or thirty years, the detailed mechanisms of how these medications affected the brain was not still clearly understood. After a while, as Jason was about to leave, Hollis' phone rang and it was Janice. Her voice was high pitched with excitement.

"Hollis, I was able to give Albert his medication and, within a half hour after taking it, his aggressiveness seems to have disappeared. The crazy look in his eyes has also disappeared. His voice sounded normal and he asked to be released from lock up. I made him suit up and let him out. He seems to be rid of the virus, or at least the effects of it."

Hollis couldn't believe what he had just heard. Was it possible that the fourth-generation antipsychotics, intended for schizophrenics had the hidden power in them to reverse the effects of the AAV virus in the brain? He was aware that pharmaceutical companies were using powerful big data analytics techniques to figure out if drugs intended for one purpose could be used for a different disease. These so called 're-purposed' drugs could be fast tracked to practical use without the normal clinical trial requirements. Was the drug Albert was taking for his schizophrenia the holy grail or the magic bullet that may work for AAV as well?

Hollis related the substance of his conversation with Janice to Jason. Jason's eyes lit up and he asked Hollis if he could take one tablet for Vicky. Hollis said, "Why not?" and got a bottle containing one hundred tablets from the wall cabinet in his office and gave Jason five tablets.

"Jason, at this time I would not advise taking these tablets as a preventive measure, just after the fact", said Hollis, as Jason thanked him and ran out of the room to go home as quickly as possible and try a tablet on Vicky. On the way home, Jason called Jamie and explained what had transpired in Hollis' office, asking her to be prepared to administer a tablet to Vicky, while at the same time warning her to be not too hopeful. What seemed to have worked for Hollis' schizophrenic brother may or may not work for Vicky.

The tablet worked for Vicky. Within two hours she was back to normal and did not need to be restrained. Jason communicated the good news to Hollis. They discussed that both for Albert and for Vicky, it remained to be seen whether the symptoms came back or were gone for good.

There were still a lot of uncertainties in Hollis' mind. He knew that continued use of antipsychotics had several undesirable side effects like weight gain and diabetes. Is one dose or two enough? Would the virus mutate so that the antipsychotics would no longer be effective? All these questions needed addressing. Suddenly there was a call from his boss at the CDC. "Hollis, look at the UN website. This news just showed up. It seems that a group of researchers in Asia had shown that third and fourth generation atypical antipsychotics, normally used for schizophrenia, worked like a miracle drug against AAV. There is just the dosage, but not much more. The report says that for a statistically significant population, this dosage worked and the subjects were asymptomatic thereafter. It is somewhat surprising that they seem to have already completed extensive trials on large human populations.

Every country has already started to administer this medication and reports from across the globe seem to confirm that this indeed works. Could it really be true that a known drug for mental illness had saved humanity from a catastrophe? No one was questioning the ethics of trials on human populations. Hollis and the rest of the world would learn much later that a team of crack scientists on the other side of the world had done the basic validation work on human subjects with two different mutations of the AAV virus. It would also be much later that a debate would be sparked on the ethics of such experiments and the conclusion reached that under special emergency circumstances, controlled experiments on human subjects with prior consent would be possible. The activities of the Project X team had not been in vain.

The schizophrenia medication was pretty widely available already, and pharmaceutical companies ramped up production of extra doses, so that within a few weeks more than enough supply was available to administer to everyone who was stricken. Fortunately, Vicky and Albert returned to normal without relapse, and relapses were very few and far between worldwide. It seemed that the virus had met its match, and had either vanished or become dormant.

Vaccine development work had started already on a worldwide scale. It would be a couple of years before a suitable vaccine could be developed. Remembering the Covid experience, this time around, with a cure in hand, pharmaceutical companies were being more circumspect in claiming success in vaccine development.

Mr. X1 addressed the meeting of all ten team members. Mr. X10 had recovered after taking the antipsychotic medication.

"We have provided the medication to all subjects of our previous tests and experiments. It is important to note that while an accident may have enabled the virus to infect humanity, it was our ability to use human subjects for discovering antidotes that quickly led to identifying atypical antipsychotics as a possible cure, and save humanity. In any case, given what happened during the last few weeks the government has decided to indefinitely postpone this line of investigation using human subjects. The project is canceled and we are being disbanded. Today is our last day here at this institute as a team. You may all go home at the end of the day. Your new assignments and jobs will be informed to you by next week. Take care and good-bye. The meeting is adjourned for the last time".

Hollis Crane visited his brother at Christmas that year. Although the antipsychotic medication worked on a permanent basis against the AAV virus, for schizophrenics it was never a permanent cure – just a medication that would keep their symptoms suppressed and under control. They would have to continue taking their tablets every day for the rest of their lives, if they hoped to remain close to normal.

Although Hollis knew that his brother would never recover fully, it did not dampen his enjoyment of Christmas with him, after many years.

LISTEN TO THE STARS

*We are but a speck in the vast nothingness of the universe —
but we are all we have, all we know*

Liz and her husband Liam had just returned from her best friend Jane's funeral. The last six months had been extremely difficult in that Jane's cancer had taken a sudden turn for the worse, and she had chosen to terminate medical intervention. Liz was the only one in a position to comfort Jane and be a friend, caregiver and counselor, all rolled into one. Although this was a first such experience for Liz, she was substantially aided in her efforts by many things she had learned from her conversation with an old man, in a far-away town, over a year ago. She remembered every detail of that meeting, and with the help of some of the old man's ideas and philosophies, she was able to bring peace and a sense of understanding, acceptance, and closure to Jane's last days.

Liz remembered that visit to San Francisco, it was just as if it was yesterday.

Her work had brought her to San Fransisco from New York. Liz had never been to San Fransisco and thought it would be a great opportunity to mix business with a couple of days of sightseeing. Her only concern was that the kids needed to be looked after whenever her husband was not available, but her in-laws, who lived not too far away, offered to help, so it became a relatively easy undertaking: arrive in San Francisco on Saturday, one day of sightseeing on Sunday, work Monday through noon on Friday, with possibly the evenings off, then one and a half days off from Friday lunchtime to Sunday morning, fly back Sunday – a busy schedule, but one that Liz looked forward to. Arriving at San Francisco airport, she quickly connected with the uber driver and settled back in her seat on way to the Grand Hyatt at Union Square where she would be staying, and the executive meeting sessions will be held. She would decide on rental car vs ride-share later, aware that parking was notoriously tough in the city. She texted her husband and her kids that she had arrived safely and they wished her a good trip.

At forty, with a trim figure, laugh lines around her eyes and a confident tone of voice, you wouldn't guess that she was the mother of two teenage kids, with a job as the marketing director for a major food chain. She was happily married to Liam Fitzgerald, a university professor. She called herself a curious optimist, always looking to the future with anticipation and a sense of adventure. In her interactions with people, she tried to find a balance between stereotyping and discovering uniqueness. Her knowledge of people from different countries and cultures made it tempting to stereotype, but her interest in human behavior and psychology helped her find the uniqueness in people.

Her room on the twenty-eighth floor offered a great view of the city as well as the Bay. In the late afternoon, she could see the Bay bridge as well as the Golden Gate Bridge, an immense spectacular vista. After a quick shower and snack, she decided to take uber and visit the Golden Gate Bridge. It was not disappointing. She had heard about it and read about it and seen the bridge in movies, but there is never any substitute for the real experience. The sunset gave a reddish-yellow glow to the city skyline on one side, while the sailboats around Alcatraz, white sails on the blue waters, defined the scene on the other. The bridge, with its reddish-brown spans was impressive, not particularly because of its size or appearance, but because it seamlessly merged with the incredible beauty of the whole scene, the skyline, the ocean, the sailboats, the seagulls, and the evening sky. It was as if the man-made bridge was necessary to complete the grandeur of nature.

Returning to her hotel, Liz decided to try one of the many French restaurants near Union Square to cap off her first night in San Francisco. She liked French cuisine and French wine, but she was not used to fine-dining by herself. Only on trips like this would she venture out to a restaurant alone. She had heard about Rue Fleur, within walking distance from the Hyatt, and decided to try it. There was only one table available and the hostess graciously let her have it. The place was cozy, the prix fixe menu had acceptable options and the wine list had her favorite St. Emilion Grand Cru Bordeaux. Everything was perfect. Liz settled into the plush leather chair and had just started to consider the different menu options when the hostess interrupted her with an unusual request.

Pointing with an open hand towards a person standing near the door, she said
"An elderly gentleman is respectfully asking if he may join you since there are no other tables available. No pressure. He totally understands if you would prefer to dine alone".
Liz looked in the direction of the doorway and saw a gentleman who was indeed elderly, in fact she would say that he looked not a day under eighty. Casually dressed, with a cane, he had a bald head with a fringe of white hair and a trimmed white beard. His skin was deeply wrinkled, and he had a slight stoop. He wore glasses and was looking in her direction with a friendly smile on his face. On an impulse, Liz agreed to let the gentleman join her for dinner. Complex thoughts went through her mind during the few seconds while she was considering the request. The man looked friendly and warm. He was so old that he would not hit on her, very likely. She was doing him a favor. She was curious about people, knew no one in San Francisco outside of her work, and this man obviously had at least one shared interest, French cuisine. She might actually find him interesting to converse with. All this raced through her mind and she found herself nodding acceptance.

Liz watched out of the corner of her eye as the gentleman slowly walked over to her table, relying on the cane for walking. It was quite possible that she had underestimated his age. Ninety? He leaned the cane against the wall and sat down opposite her.

"Thank you very much for taking a chance". He said with a disarming laugh.

He may look ninety, but his voice sounds much younger, thought Liz. Smilingly, she held out her hand and just said "Liz". He shook her hand and said "Avtar", with a twinkle in his eye.

Liz had never known anyone named Avtar, *so that itself justifies my taking a chance*, she thought. She tried to guess Avtar's ethnicity, but it wasn't easy. Avtar's deeply wrinkled face, his light brown skin, with age spots, the white hair and beard, all made his *age* the defining feature of his appearance, rather than his ethnicity.

"An unusual name. May I ask what sort of name it is and where you are from originally?"

"Avtar, spelled with two a's instead of three is just another spelling for 'Avatar', commonly known these days as an electronic image representing an internet user. You may be surprised to know that it is originally an Indian word, going back thousands of years, meaning an incarnation of God on earth. I am close to verifying my identity directly with Him pretty soon, I guess.", he said with a laugh.

Liz made a mental note to look up the origin of 'Avatar' later. She knew of the blockbuster James Cameron film as well as the sequels by that name, but not the thousands of years old origin of the word itself. She had learned something, and that made her happy. Avtar aroused her curiosity. He had a way of combining an impish sense of humor with the gravity and experience of age.

"Did you have a chance to look at the menu and do you have any questions for me?", asked the waiter, interrupting them politely, while putting a basket with a collection of breads covered in white cloth at the center of the table. They ordered their Prix Fixe options and agreed to share a bottle of Liz's favorite Bordeaux. The waiter uncorked the bottle and poured the wine, keeping the glasses only about a third full, like most good waiters know to do. Liz was tired after her long flight and visit to the Golden Gate Bridge, and she knew that the wine could make her suddenly very sleepy. She wanted to enjoy her dinner and possibly also her conversation with Avtar, so she had to be careful about how fast she drank. The waiter brought them a couple of rounds of complimentary tidbits and while waiting for the first item on the menu, Liz asked:

"Avtar, do you often dine alone in fancy restaurants like this?"

"It is a matter of perspective", said Avtar, quickly, with a smile, sniffing his wine, but not drinking it yet. Liz waited for the explanation.

"To you, it appears that I came here to dine by myself, but actually I have a perspective that is quite different. I am actually dining with everyone who is here. Just not talking with them. I consider myself strongly bonded with every human being on earth, a very fragile population on a little planet that is revolving around a sun that is one of trillions. Even multiple trillions of suns would be lost in the vastness of space. Given that scale of things, and the commonality I share with every other human being, I do not differentiate between humans who are family, friends or acquaintances and those who are not. It is just that I have not had the chance to meet these people yet, to know them yet.

When I came here, I looked around and everyone looked like someone I know quite well. The couple at the other table could be my daughter and son in law. The family of four in the table next to us could be my relative's family. Just they look different, and they have different names. I didn't know you a few minutes ago. Yet we are talking now and dining together. What is the difference between us sitting at the same table or at different tables and thinking our own thoughts, just not sharing them? Very little, certainly insignificant if you consider the scale of the universe and our existence in it".

Liz interrupted, "Hey wait, you get to know people after you have exchanged introductions and started talking with them. Surely there is a difference between total strangers and people you have started communication with?"

"To answer your question, Liz, let's look at the reverse situation. We meet people when we travel. We talk for hours sitting next to each other on a long flight or sitting at a bar. We feel we have so much in common, many shared interests, we exchange phone numbers and social media contact information, promising to keep in touch. Yet, in very few cases, do we keep up the contact. The exigencies of our lives make us focus on day-to-day activities and day-to-day people, friends, family, relatives, acquaintances, bosses, colleagues. The people we met in far-away places, people we know, become strangers. If people we know can become like strangers, people we don't know can be thought of as friends. I never dine alone, it's all a matter of perspective."

Liz was somewhat taken aback by Avtar's tirade at a straightforward observation that he came to the restaurant to dine by himself. It was going to be a long dinner. She felt like arguing a bit with the old man's screwed up logic. She was half-regretting allowing him to join her. This crazy philosophy was intriguing though, she thought.

"Wow, you certainly have an interesting and unique perspective, Avtar! but let me try and challenge it a bit more. Our concept of friends and family and people we know, is based on *shared communication and experiences*. We share and only then claim to know someone. If we enjoy spending time together, we can become friends. Are you not missing that aspect of it when you think of strangers as people you know and therefore imagine that you are not dining alone. You *are* dining alone. They are dining with their friends and relatives or colleagues or whatever. They won't talk with you any more than a cursory 'hi'. 'Alone' to me means without conversation. Conversation or communication in the broadest sense, in all its forms, is the binding factor, the glue, the very soul of social intercourse. Without conversation we are alone. Right? Are you not using this universe argument as a cop out for not having anyone to dine out with? Did you think or feel this way when you were younger? Or were you without friends then too?"

Liz knew that was a jab at Avtar's age and situation, but sensed somehow that he could handle it. It was probably the twinkle in his eyes as she was talking, that made her go on and add that last little twist. She felt that he had this conversation before with others and her comments were not a surprise. Avtar paused and sipped his Bordeaux. Liz looked down, away from Avtar's eyes, and focused on her lobster bisque. There was a loud peal of laughter from the family dining at the next table. It happens when everyone laughs at the same time after an extended period of hushed conversation.

Avtar finished his soup, and wiped his face with the white napkin with a scripted *RF* woven into a corner. Then, before the next course arrived, he waved away an imaginary fly or insect and continued.

"Liz, Liz, my dear Liz. Of course, you are partly correct. I have had, throughout my long life, the normal circle of family, relatives, friends, acquaintances, and colleagues. I understand that world. Now I am extending that concept, albeit in somewhat modified form, to all people I chance to meet or be around. Of course, there is often no conversation between me and all my imaginary friends. That is fact. Everything else is perspective. Talking about your criterion of shared experience, what can be a greater shared experience than that we were all born on the same planet, are breathing the same air, eating the same food, and *for decades* witnessing the successes and failures, triumphs and tragedies of mankind all over the world, be it in the arenas of sports, politics, natural phenomena, or entertainment, and sharing the greatest ride of all, in space, around the sun!! True, we did not sit at the same table or lived in the same house while doing so, and I don't know their names, but still we shared, did we not? Whether we converse when we meet randomly on the street, at a store, in a park or in a restaurant, is up to us. The sharing has happened, and is happening as we speak, it is real, undeniable, and on a scale that is quite grand. I am pointing out not just a logical fallacy, but the reality that our shared existence on earth is something we should pay more attention to. It is more than just a matter of perspective, it is a matter of being more inclusive, of having a broader view of reality, while still staying this side of truth."

Liz had finished her first course while trying to digest the essence of Avtar's philosophy. She had to admit that she could not quickly refute his logic, although she felt that people would laugh at her if she tried to convince them of it herself. They attended to their second and third courses, taking a sip of the Bordeaux from time to time, when Liz suddenly said,
"Can I pour you some wine, your glass is only a quarter full".
"Sure, thanks, but you could also have said three quarters empty", said Avtar with a smile.

"Yeah, but I am a positive thinker, an optimist, so for me the glass is half full, as the saying goes, never half-empty".

"Aha!" responded Avtar,

"Another good example where common sayings are not so well grounded in logic or perspective. I could argue that a positive person would say *half-empty* because that implies there is room for improvement and action. *Half-full* is a lazy person's way of looking at the situation, superficially positive, but not encouraging any action. Obviously when the phrase first became popular, people just focused on the words, *full* and *empty* and assigned positivity to one and negativity to the other, and subsequently no one questioned the logic, because the original saying is catchy and quickly gained wide acceptance.

Such is the nature of our very young civilization. Through a mere fifty generations of human society as we know it, and more intensively only in the last two or three, we have come to accept norms in all aspects of society and behavior that have been carry overs from previous generations, driven by religion and culture, and taught by parent to child, making it very hard for the next generation to question and change. When such changes have in fact happened, driven usually by a small group of independent thinkers, there is rebellion and social unrest and lawsuits that end up in the Supreme Court. Even so, both at the national and world levels, there is still not common agreement on many basic human and social issues, and this is also driven by religion, culture and politics - but then again, it's all irrelevant".

Liz had finished the escargot, the fish and the duck items, interspersed with complimentary mouth fresheners, and had to wait for Avtar to catch up. Their waiter, true to his calling, was waiting - for Avtar to finish the duck before bringing out the next item, the filet mignon. Liz was thinking how easily and seamlessly Avtar had connected a discussion on a simple saying like *the glass is half-full* to societal behavior and the learning that is handed down from parent to child. Avtar had mentioned *perspective* several times. She was rather surprised and proud of herself that she could understand most of Avtar's perspectives even though this was the first time she was exposed to them. She wondered why he had said – *but then again, it's all irrelevant.*

She began to get curious about Avtar's views on a variety of topics like religion, science and technology, politics, family and society, relationships, etc. certain that he had unusual but insightful perspectives on each of those. She was curious, too, about Avtar's background and profession. She was also aware that their dinner time together would not allow for much more time for discussion. After a while, she asked,

"Avtar, I am curious about you. What did you or do you do for a living? Have you lived in this area all your life? What brought you to this restaurant tonight?"

Avtar did not reply for a while, aware that his first responsibility was to the waiter eyeing his progress discreetly from a distance so that the next item on the menu could be brought out. The enjoyment of the delicate taste of French cuisine is enhanced more easily by sipping Bordeaux than by talking about philosophical perspectives. He would have to think about how to answer Liz's questions truthfully, completely, and concisely. It was time for the filet and it did not disappoint. It was done just right, with a peppercorn-brandy sauce that added to the natural flavor of the meat. Halfway through, Avtar put down his fork, took another sip of the St. Emilion and was just starting to answer Liz's question when the steady hum of conversation at the restaurant was suddenly interrupted by a commotion near the entrance doorway.

A homeless person, bedraggled and dirty, had suddenly opened the door and was standing inside the restaurant. The staff and customers were all staring at him as he kept saying something indistinct and incoherent. One of the staff was on the phone, and appeared to be calling the police. Everyone, staff, waiters and diners all seemed frozen in the middle of whatever they were doing and stared at the man who had just appeared in their midst. Avtar looked at the man and lip-read him as saying that he wanted water. Liz watched with surprise as Avtar got out of his chair and without taking his cane, hobbled over to the man, took out a twenty-dollar bill from his wallet and gave it to him, asking him to get water and whatever else he wanted from a nearby store. He also told him that he risked being called the police on, if he walked into restaurants like this. The man nodded, thanked Avtar and left. The whole incident took about three minutes to unfold and conclude. Avtar hobbled back to his seat, took

155

another sip of the Bordeaux and resumed his focus on the filet mignon without saying one more word. The owner of the restaurant, a portly gentleman, presumably of French origin, came over and thanked Avtar in a way that it was clear he recognized Avtar. Then he said something to their waiter and walked away. Liz and Avtar would discover later that they had gotten a twenty percent discount on their bill as a gesture of the owner's gratitude for the smooth way in which Avtar had defused and dealt with a situation that had the potential to get sticky.

While Avtar was finishing his filet, Liz spoke up:
"Avtar, you handled that situation very well. Everyone else seemed unsure of what to do."
Avtar quickly replied:
"I think of homeless people as some of my seriously underprivileged friends and I just did what seemed instinctively to be the best way to deal with the situation. I deserve no special praise or credit. My only fleeting thought was that twenty dollars helps him today, but what about tomorrow? I could get depressed if I dwelt on the homeless man's misfortunes, but then I think about all of humanity, our fragile existence on earth, and the fact that say two hundred years from now no one we know today would be around, and what would happen to the homeless man tomorrow, or for that matter to any of us, would be totally insignificant. Why two hundred? Even fifty years from now, that homeless man and you and I and Elon Musk would all be reduced *to the same common denominator:* we all lived on planet earth once upon a time. However, today we are different, fulfilling our separate living roles, and the details of what happened in the last few minutes is quite significant in the short term, although irrelevant in the longer term. We need to optimize each instant of time, deal with what we can control comfortably, and not worry too much about what we cannot control in the present or in the future. So, I find a balance between being involved and being detached. I aim to be both. It's a matter of perspective."

There were two more courses after the filet mignon, which they finished at the same time, because neither Avtar nor Liz spoke much. Then, while waiting for the last item, the Grand-Marnier souffle with berries on top, Avtar replied to Liz's questions about his profession and background.

"I live close to here, live alone, and like to eat out at French restaurants once every few weeks. This place is one of my favorites, which is why the owner knows me, as you gathered. I am twice as old as you are, if not more, judging by your looks. I have been married twice, to lovely women, have two children and three grandchildren. I have lived in several different countries for extended periods of time and consider myself to belong to all of them and none of them, I am a citizen of the world. As to my profession, I am a Professor Emeritus at a local university, but still teaching part-time. My area of expertise is the intersection of science, philosophy and religion, with a focus on understanding the history of these three pillars of our civilization as a way to thinking about the present and the future. If that sounds too complicated or heavy for you, it is. It is a lot of words, but I have already talked about some of the basic ideas during our dinner tonight, not too complicated, is it?"

Liz thought for a moment before she answered,

"Oh, no, not at all. I understood everything you said, although I may not have grasped the significance of some of your comments. Maybe if I think about it more, I will appreciate it more. I live in New York and am visiting San Francisco on a business trip. I will be here all of next week. I just arrived in town and am very tired tonight, ready to crash, with a busy week coming up. Maybe we can have a drink sometime during the week and talk some more? I would like to hear your views on different topics if you don't mind?"

They agreed to meet again mid-week after Liz finished her work, at the Hyatt where Liz was staying. She expected her work to end early. Then she would get something to eat and then plan to chat with Avtar over some coffee and dessert, if they both fancied it. It was a good plan. She was a bit surprised at herself, that she had invited an old man whom she had accidentally met and had dinner with in a restaurant, for a chat in her hotel the following week.

Their Grand Marnier souffle had arrived, with extra sauce and berries on the side. It had the right level of browning on the top, and was the perfect capping to a delicious meal. They shared the bill, appreciating the discount, shared contact information and walked out the restaurant together before parting ways.

Walking back to her hotel, Liz called Liam just as he was getting to bed, and told him about her dinner adventure. Liam was a Professor of Physics and was also very keenly interested in the overlap between science and religion. In fact, he told her that this was one of his favorite discussion topics with some of his students and colleagues, and they had formed a close-knit campus club about a year ago. They would often have a reading assignment related to this topic and then discuss different viewpoints for an hour or so with a sandwich lunch in the faculty dining room. They had named their club: The SURAM Club, for Science, Universe, Religion and Man. This was a very popular activity among a close group of students and faculty from several different departments. They were planning to broaden the club's scope and invite speakers from other Departments and Universities. He had heard about Avtar and said that Avtar was one of few faculty in universities worldwide who taught this topic. MIT, U Chicago and the University of Edinburgh in Scotland were some of the other schools which also had courses in this area. He asked Liz to write down some of Avtar's ideas and comments so that she could share it with him when she returned to New York. Liz said she would. She arrived at her hotel, said 'Good night' to Liam before getting on the elevator to her floor. After taking one last look at the Bay, with the twinkling lights on the bridges and the lights of the city surrounding the darkness of the waters, she pulled the curtains over the windows, and fell into a deep dreamless sleep on the comfortable queen bed.

Woken by her alarm at 7am, she had a message from Liam waiting for her. Liam could not resist the opportunity to meet with Avtar and was planning to visit her in San Fransisco for the last few days of her trip. He would be arriving on Wednesday and would return home with her on Sunday. He had managed to reorganize his work assignments and asked his parents to stay at their place with the kids. He was keenly interested in meeting with Avtar, and requested Liz to try to move their meeting to Thursday, if possible, since he was planning to arrive late Wednesday. Liam felt that this was a golden opportunity to talk with one of the authorities in the field on some of the topics that their lunch group often discussed and was so passionate about.

Liz immediately texted Avtar and Avtar agreed to meet Liam and her after dinner on Thursday instead of Wednesday. Liz's work schedule would decide the exact time, but it would be around 7:30, they agreed, unless Liz texted him otherwise. The week went fast for Liz. She met, for the first time, many of her company people whom she had previously only talked with on the phone or exchanged emails with. She often thought of what Avtar had said about shared experiences when she met someone new.

The person had gone through life and many experiences over the years without realizing that these experiences were actually mutually shared. It was only when they met and talked about it, did they realize what they had shared and how much. The lack of knowledge or acknowledgment of sharing did not make the sharing any less, just more hidden.

She also started to think about the earth as being a relatively small object in the huge universe rather than the entire universe of her consciousness, which was her previous way of thinking. Avtar was right in a way. Just thinking with a different perspective can change the way one looks at anything. It was also remarkable, she thought, that a chance meeting in a restaurant with an elderly professor had started her thinking in a different way.

Liam arrived as scheduled on Wednesday night. They met after Liz had finished work and went to a small sushi place in Union Square. After finishing dinner, they went back to their room and watched TV for a while. Liam was all excited at the prospect of meeting Avtar. Liam told Liz that there was a Professor at MIT who Liam had heard talk at a department seminar many years ago. He had written a book about how different people in different situations have completely different views about the passage of time. It was the human brain analog of the principle of relativity, in a manner of speaking. Also, Stephen Hawking the renowned astrophysicist had posited that to explain the origin of the big bang or the origin of life, it was not necessary to invoke the concept of a divine creator. Not that he was denying the existence of a divine creator, it just wasn't a necessary construct. Topics such as these, which lay at the intersection of science and religion had fascinated him for the last twenty or so years, and he was going to relish the chance to meet with Avtar and discuss these and similar topics further. Liz understood and supported Liam's passion.

After work and a quick dinner on Thursday, Liz and Liam waited for Avtar at the Grand Club of the Hyatt on the thirty-second floor. This lounge area, reserved for registered guests of the hotel, with its unparalleled views of the city and the bay, was the perfect setting, thought Liz, for the meeting with Avtar and discussion on esoteric topics, while drinking wine and floating far above the city of San Francisco. Avtar showed up on time and after the introductions and hand-shakes, they ordered a bottle of Silver-Oak cabernet from Napa and settled down in the comfortable lounge chairs by the floor to ceiling glass windows overlooking the city. As soon as the pleasantries were over, Liam got right down to business.

"Avtar, we understand that the course you teach is an unusual one in that it covers topics that are on the intersection of three distinct areas of knowledge: science, philosophy and religion. Can you describe some basic ideas that form this intersection or overlap, and can you share with us what are some key concepts you teach your students, or you want the students to think about"?

Avtar thought for a bit, then said just one word:

"Perspective".

Then he continued after a pause:

"If there is one concept that I would like my students to understand the importance of, and develop, it is enshrined in that one word. He repeated it for emphasis: *perspective*. I am sure you have used that word many times in different contexts and you may be wondering about the connection between 'perspective' and the intersection of science, philosophy and religion. Bear with me.

Picture your family, yourself, your wife, Liz, and your two teenage children in your house in New York. It could be any day, let's say it is 8pm. You are each thinking about the details of your lives since they are no doubt very relevant and important. Let's say for example, Liam you are worrying about a tax audit. Liz you are thinking about a discussion with your boss regarding future opportunities and also worrying about your mother's health and the two teenagers are engrossed in a conversation that only teenagers can be engrossed in. I want to let the importance, relevance and reality of this scene sink in before I take you on a little imaginary trip, to space. Imagine you are on the NASA satellite that allows you to go a hundred thousand miles away, so that you can see the earth as a round spherical object floating in space, similar to how we see the moon from the earth. Every human being on the planet is inside that little sphere. You can make out the shape of the North and South American continents, and you can imagine that somewhere tinier than a tiny dot is the State of New York and even tinier, completely invisible on this scale, is your home and there are four of you there in that home, with your problems and worries, living and thinking about the details of your lives.

There are four billion of us humans doing the same thing, thinking, doing, worrying, crying, laughing, all existing, tightly packed together, in that bluish colored sphere you see, a hundred thousand miles away. Do you begin to see your problems with a slightly different perspective? Do you realize that although your life and its problems are unique, it is hard to think of them as terribly significant any longer? That is the essence of perspective."

"You mean eight billion, right" Liam interrupted.

"No, the other four billion are sleeping, blissfully", said Avtar with a laugh.

"Let's not stop here though. Let us give ourselves eternal life and continue our travel. We are now far, far out there in space, outside our galaxy, thousands of trillions of miles away. Our entire solar system, with the Sun at its center is now just like a dot, with the earth not even separately visible. We look in all directions. We wait a billion years. We have eternal life, remember!

We see another Sun in a nearby galaxy expand and devour its planets and then die as its fuel burns out, as it is destined to happen to every sun, to every star. It can take a hundred million or five hundred million or a billion years but we can wait and watch at our leisure. Time is whizzing by us and people are living and dying on our Earth, in never ending cycles, civilizations are rising and falling. We, with our eternal life, have the benefit of a perspective that others are not privy to. We look in the direction of our Sun in the Milky way galaxy and a few hundred million years later, our sun starts to die. It gets so hot that all the water evaporates from our earth and all life is extinguished. The sun would still be getting bigger and hotter for another few billion years before actually going dark, but no future generations of earthlings will be around to see that happen. This is not speculation. This is reality. It is happening to other earths and other suns elsewhere in our galaxy and in other galaxies even as we speak. Just that there is no one actually watching it with the perspective that I described. However, our minds have limitless power to imagine. Can we not create this perspective in our imagination? Yes, we can. Just a few days ago astronomers observed a star being ripped apart by a black hole. That star could very well have a planet with life on it, like our Earth, until it was destroyed by cosmic events. We think about our problems, our tax audits, our job-related issues, our health and the well-being of our near and dear ones. They are at the same time extremely important and totally irrelevant. It is a matter of perspective. Perspective allows us to simultaneously live through the details of life every moment while realizing that we are playing this game on a scale of space and time that gives us the flexibility of assigning any level of importance we want to anything we do. It is our choice, and it is a comforting choice to have. Happiness is related to the ability to choose, and perspective gives us that choice. I am not preaching one way of thinking over another. I am just showing you that there are different ways to think. I am preaching the importance of perspective."

Liz took advantage of Avtar's pause to ask:

"This way of looking at the world may be logical, but how can ordinary people who know nothing about the scale of the universe in space and time, relate to it and find meaning in it amidst the challenges and travails of everyday life? Are there other perspectives they can more readily understand and get more balance in their thinking? Is it even necessary to have any other perspective than the one you are born with and grow up with?"

Liz looked at her husband for approval, confident that she had asked a relevant question.

Liam added, "I can see the intersection between science and philosophy, but where and how does religion come into the picture?"

Avtar looked into Liam's eyes and then Liz's.

"I will share with you a way of thinking such that you can find the answers yourselves to all the questions you have asked and even to questions you have not yet asked. Before we go into the overlap with religion, let us see if we can get a broader perspective on who we are. The first humans walked the earth a little over two million years ago. Since then, we have multiplied, born and died, evolved, and learned from one generation to the next. During these two million years, there have been about fifty thousand cycles of birth and death. That brings us to today, us talking here at the Hyatt in San Francisco. A hundred years from now, no one you see today would be alive, but we would all have been replaced by others with similar appearances and ages, and they would be talking about similar important things in their lives. A hundred years ago it was the same, different people all, but very similar interactions, and the cycles will go on. You don't have to go to outer space to gain a different perspective. My daughter took me to my favorite Yosemite Valley a couple of weeks ago. That valley was carved between five and ten million years ago, but I am observing and enjoying it now. Also, I am getting a glimpse of something that will be there a million years from now. A million years ago, to now, to a million years hence – the action of my being there to observe the scenery of Yosemite makes all these times converge, in my brain, with my perspective.

Now let me share another perspective, if I may. This one ends with my thinking that, in some sense, I will never die. *How very convenient*, you say? Hear me out.

The population of our species has been growing from just a handful a million years ago, to half a billion in the mid-seventeenth century and around eight billion today. You don't have to go out very far in space for the totality of us humans to appear as a tightly knit colony of extremely busy and industrious life, scurrying back and forth, eating, enjoying, living, dying, working during daylight and sleeping when it is dark, sort of like a colony of ants, if you graciously allow the analogy. It is not terribly far-fetched to think of us all as *one organism, a superorganism* which was born a little over two million years ago, has grown ever since, and never died, although parts of itself, individual human beings, have lived and died. The analogy, on a different scale, is that cells in our body live and die, while we live on. This idea is linked closely to what is known as the Gaia hypothesis which holds that all life forms on earth form a tightly knit, interconnected, self-supporting system. The hypothesis itself goes into a lot of scientific detail, and there are scientists who do not agree with all its tenets. I teach my students that it is not necessary to agree or disagree. It is necessary to think, to reflect, to broaden perspective. You just have to think about the fact that individuals live and die, but humanity as a whole, lives on. I have two identities, as an individual and as *part of humanity*.

This interplay between our individual, apparently independent, lives and the throbbing life of all of us combined is important to think about. Individually we lead our lives with varying degrees of interaction with others, we are concerned with our daily chores and trials and tribulations, we worry about the grand-daughter's visit to the dentist or the success of our favorite sports team, we feel terribly upset at the loss of a dear one or at other sufferings meted out to us, but if we step back and reflect, we may find peace in the thought that, as a complex system, we have survived over two million years. *Two million years.* We are an integral part of an ecosystem that *never* dies. Individuals go through birth-life-death cycles of roughly a hundred years to *enable the bigger system to live on*. It has done so for two million years. It can go on for two or more million, unless we destroy ourselves. You can honestly say to yourself, *I am part of a system that will never die.* You don't have to believe in the Gaia hypothesis or even in what I am saying. You have to just observe, think about the facts as you know them, and reflect. Look at yourself and your life from the viewpoint of a third person, or from far away, either in space or time. Think about your great grandparents and your great grandchildren as one continuum, with you at the center. Develop perspective.

Now we go on to religion. Religion has always been a touchy subject. I teach my students to focus on *why* rather than *what*. In the two-million-year history of humanity, it is only relatively recently that religion was born. *Why* were religions born? A plausible scenario is that religions were born out of a lack of understanding of natural phenomena including life and death, and ascribing such phenomena to a higher power. To spread religion, it needed charismatic prophets who had the power to command attention and generate followers. Two thousand years ago, human societies began to be formed, written modes of communication evolved and charismatic leaders arose from the masses to lead by preaching. Religion was needed to understand thundershowers or why someone fell ill, or how children were born. The prophets attributed anything unknown to a supernatural power, and laid down edicts of social behavior and made it possible for society to grow and flourish. Each cycle of life made the basic tenets of religion more sacrosanct and less questioned or questionable by logic.

Most of us today belong to one of six major religions: Christianity, Islam, Hinduism, Buddhism, Judaism and No Religion. However, you see that while religion has provided people peace of mind and comfort in times of distress, it has also been the cause of untold misery and divisiveness. Throughout the history of man, separation into groups has been the cause for perceived superiority and conflict.

It needed advances in science to begin to question of the necessity of religion. This is very recent, just during our generation. The perspectives I am talking about today were simply not available a couple of thousand years ago. People looked at the sun, the moon and the stars but were not aware that there was a universe. They felt the rain and the thunderstorms, but did not know that there was an atmosphere. They felt earthquakes, but did not know that the earth was molten rock below them. Religion was necessary then, but it has become a tradition now. Observe that there were six major religions that started a couple of thousand years ago; several minor religions started between one to two thousand years ago, but nothing of any significance in the last thousand years or so. Just minor variations of existing religions at best. Wonder why? I just gave you the answers. The birth of religions was related to ignorance and the continuation of religious thought through generations is based on what we learn at birth, otherwise known as tradition, otherwise known also as *parent to child transfer of beliefs*. As we learn more about natural laws and understand our universe better, we realize that religion is there simply because it is already there, and given the nature of humanity it will always be there, a relic of our primal origins".

Avtar paused and took a sip of the Silver Oak.

"I like the Napa Silver Oak a lot better than the Alexander Valley one", he said after a while. Avtar seemed to intensely enjoy good food and drink. Neither Liz nor Liam commented. Liam liked Silver Oak, but was not aware that there were two different vineyards associated with the wine. They decided to order some dessert. The cheesecake with kiwi topping looked interesting and they ordered two, Liz and Liam intending to share one. They also ordered a tawny port each.

Liz was thinking about what Avtar had said about the Gaia hypothesis and that, if we look at humanity as one organism, then we never die unless there is mass destruction. Our individual lives and deaths are like the cells in our bodies that live and die while the bigger and more complex organism, us, in analogy, lives on. She realized that this way of thinking would make it easier to face death. It would be easier to come to grips with the finiteness of our existence as individuals.

The port came. There was still some of the cabernet left, so they poured it into their glasses and finished it before starting on the port. Liz asked:

"Avtar, given the perspectives you are encouraging us to reflect on, do you have a philosophy, an approach, as to how we should deal with the day-to-day issues in our lives? Isn't it easy to trivialize and ignore life's details altogether if we think about the relative insignificance of any of our actions, including life and death. Also, you didn't mention God. What is your view of God and his role in the establishment of the religions? Also, the usefulness of prayer, or otherwise?"

Avtar quickly replied,

"I did not leave out God, I use *God* and *religion* synonymously because the concept of God is central to all the major religions. Religion provides a basis for belief in God. Two thousand years ago, it was necessary to think of the existence of a superhuman power in order to explain thunderstorms, earthquakes or why babies were born. Rain dances were necessary to get rainfall. God and religion were born out of necessity and live on through tradition. Most people don't realize that the original *raison d'etre* for God has become less and less tenable with science peeling away the layers of darkness and ignorance. A common question that people ask is *Do you believe there is a God?* My answer catches them off guard. I tell them that two thousand years ago I believed in God. They stop asking any more questions. Then I tell them that I have my own definition of God. To me, God is everything that I do not know and cannot know in my lifetime. So, God represents the great unknown and unknowable. God is the gap between mankind's knowledge and what remains unexplained. That is the scientific definition of God, in my way of thinking. Very few people ask the question that I want them to ask: *Do you think there is a need to believe in the conventional concept of God?* If they did ask, my answer would be that I do not see any real need to. The concept of prayer and the power of prayer is closely linked with the concept of God. One prays to God. So, prayer, God, and religion are all included in my views on religion.

Regarding your question about a philosophy to deal with the day-to-day issues of our lives, that is a broad-based question, Liz, and I will give you an equally broad-based way to think about it", Avtar replied.

"First, though, let me share another perspective, that of the perception of the passage of time. Although the first humans walked the earth a couple of million years ago, more complex society and civilizations are only about fifty to hundred thousand years old. Imagine a video lasting one hour, recording a blip when someone is born, and another blip when someone dies, starting fifty thousand years ago until today. Essentially, we are compressing fifty thousand years of birth and death into one hour. We start the video and the first thing we notice is that there is no discernible difference between the time a person is born and when he dies. If you compress fifty thousand years into one hour, a person lives for only about five seconds. Some die young, they live for one or two seconds. Some live to a ripe old age, they live for six or seven seconds. You are about forty years old, Liz, and I am close to ninety. Yet our births are just a couple of seconds apart on this scale, as will our deaths be. I have a son, a daughter and three lovely grandchildren. Just thinking about them sometimes makes me sad that I have so few days left to enjoy them and be with them. Yet even they and their grandchildren will come and go quickly while the earth lives on, while humanity lives on.

What you see on the video is real, in a way. It shows the relative ratio or fraction of our lifespan with respect to the total time our civilization has existed. If we use a different ratio, that of our lifespan to the life of our solar system, then the fraction is even smaller, much less than a millionth of a second. Yet for us, relatively brief though our lifespan may be, it is all important. Although our entire lives are just a blip in time, we have managed to expand that blip into roughly thirty thousand sleep-awake cycles. This is all we have – thirty thousand days, to do our part, live our lives, then move on. To answer your question, we need to be involved, help others, do what is needed, be part of the community we happen to be in, and try our best to be happy as we go through our allotted thirty thousand sleep-awake cycles, give or take a few. Kindness, loyalty, trust, ambition, success, failure, family, society, love, hate, any attribute or emotion you can think of are all relevant and extremely important but, at the same time, they can be viewed as totally irrelevant.".

"Wait, hang on", Liam interjected,

"You just said two completely contradictory things- how can the same thing be extremely important and totally irrelevant at the same time"?

Avtar quickly replied,

"It's just a way of looking at life. From a practical point of view, we cannot escape life, got to live it and live it as best as we can, maximize our happiness. The details of our lives are extremely important and need our focus. That is one perspective. However, if one so chooses, one could instantaneously go to a different perspective, but still with the same goal, maximize happiness. Look at this glass, with the light shining on the deep red port and its reflections on the side of the glass. I could stare into it for a long time, swirling the port and thinking about the meaning of life. You know the saying: *in vino veritas* – in wine there is truth. All the truth there ever was - can be considered to be right here.

Yet, you can snap out of it in an instant and look at ourselves from a point in space such that the earth appears as a bluish sphere, or think about a thousand years in the future or the past. You have opened your mind and heart to a different truth - instantly. In the second perspective, the glass of port is invisible, practically nonexistent. Even the city I am in, with its millions of people, is terribly insignificant, practically invisible. However, these perspectives are not contradictory, they coexist, they are all reality, just different views of it. The dictionary defines 'perspective' as: *a way of regarding something; a point of view*. You can simultaneously look at the stars and the earth below your feet. The stars twinkle and tell. They carry the message of time, the birth of the universe, and the birth of humanity. They show you the future and the past simultaneously. The stars are telling you truths that you never knew existed. They are singing the eternal cosmic song, more powerful than any God or any religion or anything you can think of, because it includes everything, contains everything, and it is all real. You can *listen to the stars,* to the timeless message they are sending us, and also be close to the earth, close to the details of your lives, at the same time!"

After that impassioned plea to listen to the stars, Avtar was silent for a while. So were Liz and Liam. Then Liz spoke up:

"Avtar, let me change the topic. I know that you teach university students, but do you have any thoughts about children's education, pre-college?", asked Liz, thinking about her own children.

"Again, this is just my perspective and it may surprise you", began Avtar.

"For the past several centuries, the focus of education has been *learning*. We learn history, geography, literature, science and mathematics. We learn which empires dominated during what periods of time. We learn the names of continents, mountain ranges and cities. We learn the rules and principles of physics, chemistry, biology, mathematics. We learn how to write, how to draw, how to play and how to live. We live our lives learning, and we die learning. We respect the learned among us, and look down on those who did not have the benefit of learning. This was all well and good, eminently reasonable, but only until recently. Learning was important in the past when information needed to be passed down from parent to children or teacher to student or expert to apprentice in any area.

We have gone beyond that phase. Learning is still important in many areas, but less in others. The advent of the information age makes all types of information available to us at the click of a mouse. I can tell professionals things they do not know in their fields, just by looking up the relevant information in a search engine. The other day, I surprised my doctor by telling him an alternative possible diagnosis for the pain in my lower abdomen, which he had not considered. Learning facts has become *passe*. Anyone can look up anything, on any subject. What we need to develop, instead, is the ability to *analyze*. Given a set of facts, what conclusions can we draw? What do those facts really mean? What can we predict will happen? The power of thinking, of analysis, has been stifled in us by the pressure to learn facts. One of the iconic companies of this country, IBM, has a one-word motto that has been its slogan and motto for over a hundred years. That word is THINK. It is not LEARN. Companies like Google or Amazon hire people not based solely on what they know, but more based on how they approach and solve problems they are given at their job interviews. So, in answer to your question, Liz, I would encourage children to analyze more, to think more, to make connections, to try to predict, not just learn facts. Children's education should stress their ability to think. Children's toys should make them think - *why*" and children's books should have examples of the questioning mind, of making connections, of asking more often *why* rather than *what*. The nursery rhyme *Twinkle Twinkle Little Star* has become timeless because it reduces children and adults to the same common denominator of wonderment.

There was a long silence as Liz and Liam looked at each other.

The cheesecake with the kiwi on top was delicious. They ordered another round of the tawny and then Liam asked,

"Avtar, changing topics again, at our school we had an animated discussion recently on the pros and cons of mass media. What are your thoughts on this subject? I am sure our students and faculty would be interested."

They waited for Avtar to finish sipping his port.

"The development of science and technology, in the broadest sense, happened because we sought to understand natural phenomena and the physical world around us. It was not one event, but a long series of interconnected discoveries and accomplishments over the last few hundred years. It includes not only our knowledge of the laws of science but also our understanding of physiology and medicine and, recently, the gene and its role in human evolution. It is based on a way of thinking that leads to an almost endless chain of discovery and validation, followed by prediction and then new discoveries and new validations. Although the technologies that enable mass media came from the knowledge base of science and technology developments, the actual use, influence and power of mass communication goes far beyond the confines of science and technology. It is as if a proverbial genie, that has the power to change the *mind* of humanity, has been released from the bottle.

The internet and social media are enabled by the technology of data storage and data communication. The next big thing is artificial intelligence, for which again the enabler is technology that allows storage and processing and transfer of data on a scale that was incomprehensible only a couple of decades ago. In discussions with my students, we usually end up by agreeing that some of the negatives of easy and instant mass interconnectivity and mass communication are a difficult challenge for this and the next generation."

Liam jumped in: "We typically assume that easier communication and interconnectivity is all positive. Families separated by distance can see each other when they chat. Meetings can be held virtually, and we can disseminate information much more widely than previously possible.

Mass communication is so much easier these days than what it was fifty years ago. Can you say more about the negatives?"

"Sure, but let me first define what I mean by mass communication. I mean all mass media, TV included. When I was young, children did not watch much TV. We read books and newspapers and once in a while watched movies on the big screen, in theaters. Old fashioned, yes, but rewarding. When we read books, we could stop and think about what we read. When we watched movies in theaters, it was fun to relax and let our minds be under the control of the director of the movie, and let our thinking follow the pace he set. Every time we watch TV, we think at someone else's pace. We have become used to this. We have little time to reflect, absorb, debate, and then continue. A book acknowledges that our brains work differently, at different speeds, with different levels of interpretation. A show on TV, to a large extent, forces all viewers to the same common denominator, to think and follow the storyline at the same pace, with not much regard for individual differences in ability, inclination or attitude. Is this good or bad? Positive or negative? You be the judge. I am just pointing out the differences.

Next, let's talk about what we loosely call social media. When we talked about religion, I told you that we have not started any totally new religion in the last thousand years. Maybe that is not completely accurate. If you look at how social media is being used or misused today, it has similarities to the spread of religion a thousand years ago. Let us consider the defining features of religion. A charismatic, messianic individual who has millions of followers, explains events happening around them, warns of danger and promises a better future. He casts himself and his followers in the role of saviors, and all others as destroyers. He has the ability to incite rebellion and violence just by the power of his speech. Truth and facts take a distant second place to hype and the ability to persuade. He claims God is on his side and he is the de-facto personification of this 'god'. He could be a political figure, a movie celebrity or a billionaire, and in some cases a combination of the three. His followers are blind, they do not question him much. They are prepared to go the distance for him. They form a sub-group and repeat and spread his sayings among them. Different groups have different leaders and different, often opposing viewpoints. Sounds similar to how social media influences the lives of people, does it not?

All the above could be used to define the inception of any of the major religions, and also the cult-like following some people have on social media today. What is worse, is that our legal system has not quite caught up with the potential evils of a privately owned social medium platform with billions of followers. The God of a billion followers has us at *his* mercy!", Avtar said with a laugh.

"Of course, no analogy is perfect, but you get the picture, I trust. So, what is the problem with the above scenario? Over the course of the last hundred years, our human society has had so much reliance on the development of science and technology that we have become accustomed to logic and truth and facts as the unquestionable guiding principles of our lives. We have come to regard anything that is not based on facts or truth to have no place in our daily discourse, that is, until recently. It amazes me that often no matter how blatant or obvious a lie is, if someone who is a 'media God' propagates it, it is regarded as gospel by his followers. Attempts to 'prove' its falsehood are at best minimally successful within the follower group. When people outside the group challenge the followers with facts and proof, they are simply told that the facts are wrong, that everyone is lying. The very foundations of science and logic are being questioned. We have a conflict between free speech and truth, between free speech and incitement, between free speech and hate speech – and this is enabled by technology, coupled with our social justice and legal system that allows private control."

"How can society prevent it?", asked Liz

Avtar quickly replied: "Legislation! Money and power have been synonymous over the centuries. Now it is the triad of money, power and technology. Nothing wrong with that, unless it translates to the potential to harm people by spreading misinformation under the guise of free speech.

Technology created the problem, and a combination of technology and smart legislation can fix it.

Think about it: today the power of social media to spread the views of a small group of people, is limitless. Perhaps we should go in the direction of intelligently limiting it.

I have given you a practical answer to your question, but if you ask me if I spend sleepless nights worrying about evil gods controlling our mass media, I will tell you that I don't. I sleep well every night. Although the conflict of mass communication with the so-called right of free speech needs to be addressed, and I do believe there is a great potential of harm to individuals as well as mankind, I think it is nothing to get too worried or uptight about. If you recall my philosophy of being involved and being detached, of simultaneously regarding the details of life as extremely important and totally irrelevant, the existence of the social media religious cult is at the same time concerning and also irrelevant, in the broader scheme of our existence. Going back to my favorite perspective, looking at the Earth as a tiny blue sphere from space, it is not all that concerning what one percent of the earth's population is thinking or doing during the five seconds of their existence, relatively speaking, as long as they are not bent on destroying the other ninety nine percent. Armed with the ability to view life from a different perspective, you may find it easier to relax about many of the pressing social topics of the day, be they connected with race, religion, sexuality or women's rights, or even crypto (with a smile).

Think about it - we are not much different from billionaires. The rulers of countries or kingdoms and the Gods on social media are not much different from the homeless man on the street or the criminal locked up in jail. *Five seconds,* and we will depart - that is the difference, that is the beauty of perspective."

They sat in silence for a while, then Liam asked,
"Avtar, we have talked about a perspective that looks at mankind as one super-organism that was born millions of years ago and will never die unless it destroys itself. You mentioned some ways we can destroy ourselves. Could you elaborate on that a bit?"

"First let us consider what cannot destroy us. War, even nuclear war, can decimate us, destroy our civilizations, but not extinguish us as a species. We will survive, mutate and evolve, and a thousand years hence still be here. A collision with an asteroid can kill a billion people, or two, but it will not wipe us out unless the collision causes the earth to change its orbit in a way that it will either crash into the sun or go sailing away into the deadly coldness of interstellar space. Disease and viruses can kill many but I cannot imagine it killing us all before we have managed to become somewhat immune and discovered new vaccines. In short, death, even on a super-massive scale, will not extinguish us as a species. So that leaves us only two ways in the near term, that is before five hundred million years when our sun will start to die. One is loss of our environment or atmosphere, and the other is being taken over by a hostile alien civilization. The second one we cannot much control. The first one we can control to an extent but we are not united about our approach to it – we need to be. Climate change has become a buzzword. It will not seriously affect anyone you or your children will ever know. We could completely ignore and avoid the subject as individuals – but if we are to survive as a species, even a half to one million more years, we need to start seriously addressing it within the next couple of generations. The world today has just barely started thinking about problems that affect our species, as opposed to problems that affect individuals, societies and countries."

Avtar paused, took a couple of sips of the port, and asked to use the toilet. During the brief interlude, Liz and Liam discussed the possibility of Liam's inviting Avtar to a department seminar out East. When Avtar came back, without waiting for Liz or Liam to ask anything, he started off:

"Let me share another perspective with you - my thoughts about death. I am eighty-six years old. As I have aged, and observed life around me, I can see that all my college friends and relatives have aged too. Many have stopped aging - they have passed away. I have been in a position to observe death on multiple occasions, in different forms, for different people. I have had the opportunity to reflect on death and dying more than most people, simply because I have lived long.

If I take any one person and follow his life over the past seventy years, I can see the effects of the passage of time, of aging, the ravages of time as they say. However, another way to look at life is to observe a space and watch the people filling that space. If I do that, I see that my students have not aged. Pretty surprising, eh? They change their names and appearances every year but remain the *same age*. For the last many decades as I walk in to the classroom, I see the same young faces. Not just my students, everywhere I go it is the same thing. The Starbucks cashier has not aged one bit in the last thirty years, neither has the gas station attendant or the bank teller. This perspective makes me realize that youth is constantly replenishing age, life is constantly replacing death. I have aged as I have lived and I will pass on soon, but they will always be there, always the same age, in the classrooms and gas stations and coffee shops of this world, walking by the lake or by the river or hiking some trail, for millennia to come.

Death is just like extended dreamless sleep. We have no consciousness of our bodies or the passage of time. The only difference is that we wake up from sleep. One day my consciousness will be extinguished when I die, but in the broader context, I will live on – not just through my children and grandchildren, but through all of humanity.

We are used to death being totally a cause for sadness, for mourning, with nothing good to say in its favor. We live our lives trying our best to avoid death. By and large it is a success story because we always succeed in avoiding death, failing but once. We have found many ways as a society to make death less painful, more bearable. We talk about angels, heaven, meeting our forefathers, being free of burdens, going to the great beyond. We try to avoid using the word *die*. People pass away, they seldom die. We often don't even mourn death any more, we *celebrate the life* of someone who has died. When a younger person dies, it's because *those whom the gods love, die young*. We try our best to put a positive spin on death.

My perspective is different: I do not really die. This is not semantics, but reality. Of course, as I mentioned before, my consciousness is extinguished, and my body will turn to dust, but even as I will breathe my last breath I can see, hear and feel living people all around me. *I am them. They are me.* We are part of the same humanity. A miniscule part of humanity is dying with me, but in the main, I will live on through them, easily, merrily, permanently."

Liz remembered when her grandmother passed away. Just before she closed her eyes, she had looked around the room, and seen her near and dear ones gathered around her, and she had a peaceful smile on her face. She may have felt a sense of this continuation of life – who knows?

"Avtar, we have talked about your perspectives on a lot of different topics including death, do you have some unique advice on *how to live life* for those of us who cannot visualize going out to space and looking at earth as a tiny bluish sphere?", asked Liz with a smile.

"I am not in the business of doling out advice. Everything I have talked about is to be taken in the spirit of an old man's perspectives, just that and nothing more. I can share with you how I think" said Avtar.

"My overall goal is simple – maximize my happiness. This is not as selfish as you may think. Making others around me happy, be they family, friends, acquaintances or strangers, makes me happy too, so I do that consciously. I don't think too much about the past or too far into the future. I try to optimize my life within a plus-minus six months to a year window of time. This is a constantly sliding window. If I can be happy within this window of time, I am pretty sure I will be happy for a long time. At my age, my past is much longer than my future can be, but I don't dwell on the past. I look forward more than backwards. My future is actually more exciting than my past, always.

When things happen that are clearly negative, I try to find even the slightest positive in that happening. In dealings with people, I more often than not put myself in their shoes. This often helps me get less upset with their contrary habits or behavior. I don't think in terms of right and wrong, or black and white. I ask *why*. Very often the answer to *why* is more important than something being right or wrong.

If I truly understand why someone said something or did something, whether it is right or wrong becomes a matter of someone else's judgment criterion. It becomes a question of logic vs morality.

Oh, and finally, as often as possible, I try to *listen to the stars* and to the *sound of water*."

"*Listen to the stars*, I understand from your previous explanation, but *sound of water*?" questioned Liam.

"There is something primal in us, going back millions of years – we came from the oceans and there is magic in the sound of the waves crashing on the seashores of the world, there is magic in waterfalls, in rain, or even in the hushed murmur of a creek or river. In the sound of water there is a resonance with our very being. It connects us with our past, just like the stars do. It makes me peaceful and happy in otherwise troubled times."

The three of them sat silently for several minutes. The lounge had nearly emptied, except for a young couple sitting by the window with their arms around each other. Then Liam said,

"Avtar, Liz and I really appreciate you sharing your philosophy of life with us. I would like to invite you to visit our school out East and give a seminar. I am sure our students would love to hear from you."

"Sorry Liam, I have stopped traveling long distance, but I will be very happy to talk via Zoom or some other meeting app."

"OK, deal, you will get an email from me with the invite. We can decide on time and date and such details later", Liam happily responded. With that they decided to call it a night.

As they were walking out of the lounge, suddenly Avtar's phone rang. Avtar looked at it with a puzzled expression, then said with a laugh:

"That was an alarm, reminding me that tomorrow morning I have to tell the handyman working on the front door of my house that I would like a different design for the door handle. The one he had proposed earlier was too traditional. It doesn't match the rest of the house. Look at this picture – don't you think that this design is too old fashioned? How about this one? Or this? I have to think about which of these two I want finally – important decision, because the door gives any visitor the first impression about the house."

With that he waved good bye and hobbled to the waiting elevator. Liz and Liam smiled at each other, shook their heads, and went back to their room.

It was a full-moon night and the reflection of the moonlight on the waters of the Bay, together with the twinkling lights of the city, seemed to provide a magical merging of the unreachable distances of space with the tangible details of our civilization. The words of Avtar rang in their ears, *"Listen to the Stars, and the Sound of Water"*, deftly connecting the vastness of the universe with life on earth.

CPSIA information can be obtained
at www.ICGtesting.com
Printed in the USA
BVHW031544060423
661881BV00002B/4/J